Descending Angels

Maximilienne Montana

Published by Maximilienne Montana, 2024.

DESCENDING ANGELS

First edition. August 27, 2024.

Copyright © 2024 Maximilienne Montana.

ISBN: 979-8227115928

Written by Maximilienne Montana.

Table of Contents

Chapter One

"Malach! Join me, won't you?" I felt an assurance and calmness as they looked at me from afar. Suddenly there was a bright light. My body jolted in vigor as if somehow it was only a thing. *What is that word the humans call it? They see these things at night called what?* I could only ponder for a moment until...

"Malach buddy! What are you still floating here for!" They made my body jolt like the vision did, but only this time was different. I turned to see Sariel in front of me.

"Sariel why would you do that? Why would you umm..."
"Why would I 'scare' you like the humans call it?"
"Yeah, that is what I meant."

Sariel looked me up and down as I looked at them in silence. We were angels as God called us. The almighty beings whom humans gained what they call "comfort" from. We protect them from evil and demons or at least the angels above me do. They were chosen to be humans' guardians and guide them to their destiny. Sariel was among the high angels that got chosen to look upon these humans in their form while we low angels could not.

"Malach? Light to Malach?" They waved their white hands in the air to awaken me from this strange state. I glanced at them with a weary look in my eyes. This "mind" of mine was truly troubled.

"What visions do humans have?'

"Visions? Clarify what you mean."
"Those things they have at night when they do what they call sleep."

"You mean dreams." I nodded my head in agreement with them. "Dream is kind of like a vision, but more."

"More?"

"The young humans think of unicorns or dinosaurs that they believe are alive in their dreams."

My mind was even more troubled. *Unicorns? What is a Unicorn? Dinosaurs are correct as they lived long ago before God decided to the grand plan of humans. God decided to kill them off to create a new "species" as it commands.* Sariel continued to speak.

"Sometimes other ones think of getting what they can not have from the dream."

I responded by saying, "What can they not have?"

"It is different for each human, but mine dreams of wanting a child."

"A child would be nice for her. May God bless her with a child."

"May they."

Sariel and I nodded in unison of prayer. We started to fly over our home called heaven. Everything around us was as pure white as we were. As one would say, it meant to be pure in every way possible. Not one of us was different from the next yet it didn't feel that way. Some viewed us low angels as a disgrace to the angelic "species." Most low angels do not know the terms some high angels use. Sariel teaches me this language and disagrees as they say with the other high angels.

We continued flying over the white "clouds" that can be heard once a soul enters heaven for their eternal life. Sariel always had us fly over the almighty entrance to see new souls. The entrance was one of the only colored pieces in heaven. It was gold coloring, but the entrance itself changed depending on the soul entering.. The soul could choose what they "imagined" was the entrance to heaven. Most chose a high tower gate with statues of angels around. I never knew why and pondered it while flying. Flying allowed my troubled mind to be free. No one must ever say the word free to the archangels. It was as the humans say "forbidden." Souls entered through a black pit from the ground of heaven. Granted the ground was also white like everything else in heaven yet it had little ripples running through it that led the way toward the entrance.

I started to listen to the world around me. The usual singing from high above was present, but my troubled mind turned to the souls entering.

One soul said, "Heaven! It was true! My dreams came true!" Each soul entered with their desired clothing on.

Another soul stated, "My mother's dress! How wonderful it is to see it again! I shall never forget her loving face. Is she here? Mother! Mother, where are you?"

Many wanted to see their "parents" which I believe is the correct term they use. Most may never see them yet never feel saddened by that. Each human who entered could never feel sadness but only joy. They could never leave and are allowed no free will. They became like angels who were the purest of them all yet had no choices. The humans could see the angels flying over.

"Angels! Am I on some drugs or something? Did I hit the crack too hard? This must be some kind of trip I am having! Yo! Angel up there!"

They were yelling at Sariel and me as we were flying over. Most angels ignore the souls, but I did not. I flew down to the soul as Sariel followed me.

I asked, "Soul, what may I assist with?"
The soul responded, "Dude! Where am I?"
"Heaven soul."

The soul looked around in amazement at the place they were at. His eyes widened at the thought of heaven. This was a usual response I got to telling each soul.

He asked, "Am I dead? Did I hit that crack too hard?"

I responded, "Yes you are dead, but in heaven to spend your eternal life here."

"How did I die?"

Angels could see how a soul had died yet most did not want to, or most did not waste their moment.

"Soul, you overdosed."
"I hit that crack too hard?"
"Hit that crack?"

"I did! Dude what an amazing trip it must have been! Thanks, man!" He held out his fist and I stared in wonder at him. He took my hand and made a weird shape and hit it against his. The soul moved along. Sariel stared at me in disbelief at what we just encountered. We continued on our way.

"What did he mean by hit that crack?"

"Malach, even I do not know what he meant by hitting the crack. My human has never 'hit that crack' before." My troubled mind decided to not inquire further about "hitting the crack" even though it was still intriguing.

We continued to fly over to do our daily singing. Many angels would float by each other in silence while they listened to the above. The above is where our daily singing would commence before the daily meeting heard by the Archangels. They were almighty like us yet had different duties than us. Hierarchy was the basic structure of heaven. God was at the top and could command anything they wanted. They created us for "entertainment" as some say. Principalities, also known as Princes, were told to make sure no undestined harm came to communities or as they call "units." Units were people or groups chosen by God to be protected. There were some rumors that the Princes failed at protecting a woman named Amelia Earhart traveling around the world, yet she somehow died. Though God did show their wrath as the singing stopped for a whole cycle! The last were the Archangels that kept us high and low angels in control yet never treated us low angels with "respect" as they call it. Most low angels do not know what "respect" means and are shunned by it. Everything was always in order here in heaven and never seemed to change. Sariel was very quiet as we flew.

"Sariel?"

"Yes, Malach." They looked at me with a dreaded look in their eye. Even we angels could have feelings that were cosmic compared to humans which is why they did not happen very often.

I responded to them by saying, "Are you feeling something?"

Sariel said, "Yes, my human is in distress, and you know that I can feel her despair more than she can. We are just connected."

"What is she in despair about?"

"I am not sure, but it hurts her physically and emotionally."

"You must go to her and find out why."

"I shall and will hear about the daily meeting later when I return."

Sariel nodded goodbye and floated away leaving me alone on my way to the daily singing and meeting. My troubled mind started to wander. *How are high angels and humans connected so strongly? I wish I could be connected to one. I am not supposed to wish for anything, but I do. I want their life and experiences and to feel that connection to someone like that.* Suddenly my eyes went black, and light flashed before my eyes.

There was a strange figure in front of me smiling. They were white like all the angels, but there was a pin on their clothing that had changed color. *That can not be right! All our pins are white except the Archangels.* The pin switched between colors, and I looked into their face. I felt that assurance and calmness again. Their hair was long, and their eyes were grey like mine. Their smile comforted me. *Comfort? I knew the meaning right away without pondering. Who is this angel?* The angel opened their mouth and spoke, but I heard nothing yet still saw their smile until light blinded my eyes again.

I suddenly awoke again floating in the same spot. *That comfort I felt. It was cosmic like other emotions. They were an angel, but who are they? I know the word comfort now and understand it fully. How can I understand it? It's the work of sin again! I must purge this from my troubled mind!*

I flew the rest of the way to the above to start the daily singing. This was a time when all angels including Archangels and Princes got together to sing in joy to the God above. Some say it is there when we sing, but others say not. Only Archangels and Princes can see God in the light, yet some have seen God in its true form, but that is only a rumor. We angels love to talk or "gossip" like humans say about other angels. It is our form of entertainment like God has theirs.

I made it to the entrance of the above. When floating into the above it looked like a hole in the sky kind of like the pit where the souls entered from. There was a light ring around the hole that shined brighter every time an angel entered, but dimmed when an angel left. When entering all an angel had to do was float up or down to enter and exit. As I floated up the light ring shined a bit brighter. Once I entered most angels were silently talking to one another about the song or talking about the lower angels. As I was floating toward my spot, I overheard some angels speaking. One angel said, "How can low angels survive in heaven all day?" The other angel said, "I know! These low angels are an "abomination" to the world. My human thinks about abominations all day long." This was a typical conversation heard during this time, but I knew better than to believe them. Humans had no idea of the happenings in heaven as they were just lonely souls entering.

Suddenly there was a huge chime that rang out in the above. Like everything in heaven, the above was all white, but the angels floated on the "clouds" and there was a bright blinding light above. We all moved to our spots as the Archangels and Princes came down from the light. On all of them were pins with different colors that signified their purpose on Earth and in heaven. They nodded in unison to us as we did back to them to signal, "Hello." We all started to sing "How Great Thou Art." I sang:

> "Then sings my soul, My Saviour God, to Thee,
> How great Thou art, how great Thou art."

Each voice was as angelic as the next and yet always the same. I knew all the words and never had to try to remember them, so I let my mind wander. *We always sing about how great God is. Will I ever see their true form? Will I ever speak to them? I wish they would speak to us. I wish for this in my mind only.*

We finally finished and suddenly Gabriel, an Archangel, spoke out to us. "Welcome angels to our daily meeting! God above welcomes you." All of us nodded our heads in unison to the blinding light above to welcome God. Gabriel continued to speak and said, "God nods their head back to us. They signal us to remember our duties as they are almighty and needed to keep order. So let us pray to our God above and give them thanks for what great purpose they provide us. We must..."

Gabriel continued on, but I never listened to them speak. It was the same at every meeting, but the song would always change. My next event after the meeting was reading the bible to continue growing my purity. I could not feel "bored" like humans yet somehow, I wanted to. *I wish to feel boredom in a cosmic way sometimes.* My eyes saw a blinding light again and suddenly I saw that angel, yet we were in the above.

Their eyes looked over at me while Gabriel spoke. Most angels never smiled during the daily meeting to show they were listening, but this one did not. They smiled and looked only at me, and I looked only at them. It felt like a cosmic feeling that was glowing outside of me. This feeling was different than the comforting one. It was different than anything else I had felt before. I wanted it to stay with me forever. *I wish for this feeling and only this one.* There was suddenly a thought in my mind. Some angels could project thoughts into others, but only the "gifted" high angels could. The angel said, "Malach, I want to be free with you and only you. Join me, won't you?"

Chapter Two

The light blinded my eyes again and suddenly I wondered where I was. The angel figure had disappeared and I was floating while hearing the archangel Gabriel speak again. My eyes shifted back and forth around the area as I saw wings in front and around me. *I am in my normal spot at the daily meeting. Gabriel is speaking and no other angel is looking at me, so does this mean I am safe? What work of sin would do such a thing as this?* This troubled mind of mine could not keep up with these thoughts. Suddenly the chime rang out from the light above to signal the end of the meeting as well as the cycle. A new cycle had started and it was time to continue with the events that grew our purity.

I stayed in my spot while the angels floated past one another leaving the great above. The clouds shifted back and forth as the angels floated quickly. It was very slight, but little glowing white particles would come up from the clouds each time an angel floated past it. Lines of little glowing particles would show the trail of an angel. Some never noticed it, but I did and thought it was quite beautiful. My troubled mind was filled with dangerous thoughts, but sometimes it was filled with beauty. *Sin. Sin is a dangerous thing. Growing our purity is the most important thing yet it is not beautiful. How could something so important not be beautiful? These white particles are beauty. The above is beautiful and so are souls. They shimmer if you look just right. I wonder if humankind is just as beautiful as their souls.*

My thoughts were broken as soon as Gabriel floated towards me. "Malach, how are you?" They floated in an upright position to show they were almighty. Instead of a toga-like the rest of the angels wore, they had on armor, but their pin was blue instead of white to signal they were a protector of us all. Their hair was shorter than mine but parted to the left above their face.

"I am just as pure as I could ever be." I touched their shoulder to let them know my appreciation for their question. They nodded back in acceptance.

"You must know that if any sin comes your way, we Archangels are trained by God in the light to handle such matters." Their eyes shifted back and forth as they were saying this. It was almost as if they were focused on something else or meant it in a different way.

"I thank you for the consideration of being such a wise Archangel." In my mind, I had other thoughts on this matter. *Gabriel looks down upon us. Yet after every cycle, they come to me to ask if I am alright. They seem sincere yet are not as I can tell they are lying. We angels are not meant to lie as it is impure, but are Archangels allowed? If they are then it would make sense for the rumors of God being present or not at the daily meeting. Sometimes I wish to lie.*

Gabriel put their hand on my chest which awoke me from my thoughts. The hand moved from the right side to the left side of the chest. I looked up at their face and suddenly things got serious. It was almost as if they knew my thoughts about wishing to lie like them. "God and I know that like every other angel you are just as pure as the next. You never wish for anything outside of God's intentions." *If only they knew.* "So thank you for being such a..."

Suddenly another Archangel joined Gabriel and me. "Malach! I have been meaning to speak with you on some pure matters." Gabriel took their hand off my chest quickly and put it on their chest clutching the armor they wore. It was almost as if Gabriel was frightened by the sudden interruption.

Gabriel moved their body toward the Archangel. "Jophiel. What a wondrous sight to see you in the above. You just missed the daily meeting like you do every cycle." Their face turned into a cold look. I could not describe it as I knew not the words to use. *There is much tension in this space. I almost believe it best to hurry to my next event.*

Jophiel responded to Gabriel saying, "Ah yes, Gabriel." Their face turned from a smile in my direction to a serious face and tone toward Gabriel's direction. "What a wondrous sight it is to see you here. I imagine you continue to follow God blindly at every possible moment. Never missing an order."

"I do as the rest of us should, like God wants..."

"You mean as they command." Jophiel interrupted.

Gabriel started to speak saying, "Well, yes as they command all of us to do. With the utmost..."

"...positive intentions that God could ever want for us. We shall follow them as they are almighty above us all." I could not believe what I just heard. *An Archangel cutting off another! Especially Gabriel! No one ever cuts them off as they are the most respected. I could feel a cosmic emotion of joy, which I learned from Sariel while passing by the souls, starting to emerge, but I held back this sudden emotion. It was not the right moment for it.*

Gabriel shifted once Jophiel stopped. Their pin started to slightly turn a different color. I noticed small glimmers of red shimmering through the blue, but only for a second. Gabriel turned toward me and said, "Malach, I shall see you at the next daily meeting. May God continue to grow your purity." I nodded in their direction as they floated away, leaving a small trail of those glowing particles. Jophiel turned back to me.

"Shall we continue, on Malach?" I nodded in acceptance. Jophiel and I always met after the daily meeting even though I should go read the bible. They help me understand the words I have heard from the angels during that cycle. As we were floating, Jophiel motioned for me to start talking.

"That was wondrous! I almost felt cosmic joy in the moment! The way you stopped Gabriel from their speech was amazing." For the first moment, a smile appeared on my face, which did not appear often. I had a marking on the right side of my cheek every time I smiled which was different from the other angels.

"It was pretty joyous was it, not? I enjoy watching Gabriel shift as they speak when I know exactly what they say. It was jubilant!"

"Jubilant? What does this mean? Is it like the word joy we sing during the daily singing?"

"Almost, Malach. It is what the humans say when they feel happy or at least a version of it."

"Happiness. How can you tell if a human or their soul is happy?"

"They smile like you did just a moment ago and show their teeth while also sometimes laughing."

"I want to laugh like the humans do."
"You can. Many angels like you do not know that we are much like humans."

This thought made me ponder the views some angels had of humans. *Why are angels so hard on humans? If what Jophiel says is true then we are just like them. They are not so different. We are not so high above them as some angels think. Humans and angels can be equal and maybe we can become like them.*

"Malach, what did you learn today while passing by the gate?"

"Well, there were many souls calling out for their parents, but there was one that said something about crack? The phrase was 'hitting the crack' and Sariel knew not what it meant."

"Crack is an interesting term. It is a thing that humans use at times to get high."

"High? Like, become high angels? Are our high angels hitting the crack to become high? Is that how I can become high too?"

Jophiel smiled and laughed a bit even though I did not understand why they were laughing. They shook their head at me in response to what I said. "It is not the same term. Humans feel different when they get high. We angels use the term high as a way to distinguish high and low angels, but they hit the crack to become high or to feel something. Sometimes it makes them feel better or worse. Only humans know why."

I nodded as I was trying to understand what Jophiel just said. "So high angels do not hit the crack to become high. They are chosen. Yet humans hit the crack and become high to feel something. The feeling is the difference between our highs."

Jophiel nodded and smiled since I finally understood what they meant and we continued flying toward the entrance to the below, or heaven. I wanted to ask more before I left Jophiel until the next end of the cycle. "Before I go I need to know one thing."

"Anything. Remember I am here to help show you the beauty of humankind."

"Well, something strange has been happening. It is almost like sin, but I am not sure."

"What is it?"

"They are visions or dreams and they started happening. I see another angel that wants me to be..." I moved closer toward Jophiel to whisper it. "...free with them."

Jophiel nodded and somehow I thought they already knew who I was talking about. They did not have a concerned look like any other Archangel would when hearing about sin. "If this happens again I want you to come see me right away. Come to the above at any moment when it happens again. We will need to discuss this further."

I understood what they meant and promised I would. I nodded goodbye to them as I floated down through the entrance to the below. The light ring dimmed as I exited. I knew I needed to go and start reading the bible as I was a moment late already. While I was floating I noticed the world around me. Everything was like a cloud but they moved in the shape an angel wanted them to. The white glowing particles were not present here, but some cloud puffs were. As an angel moved the cloud, the puffs would rise up into the air until they hit the above and became part of that big cloud. I liked moving them around to make different shapes, but not everyone did that. My eyes suddenly went black and a light started to shine through my eyes.

The angel was in front of me smiling next to one of the white clouds. "Malach, come imagine what these clouds look like." My body moved toward theirs and looked above and saw some cloud puffs forming different shapes in the air. They turned to me and spoke again. "We are like humans. Cloud gazing at the sky and imagining different shapes." They pointed toward the puffs. "That one looks like a snake. An animal that is down on Earth. Malach look! That one is like a bird. They fly in the sky with the clouds and are almost like us."

I could not help but smile at the thought of imagining things in the above. *Wait! Why am I smiling at them? This is the sin again! Yet this feels nice and calming again.* They moved closer to me and suddenly I felt their hand on mine. My face turned toward theirs and they were closer than I thought. Inches away from my face as they smiled and yet somehow my face smiled back at theirs. The calmness started to fade away and was replaced by something else. I knew not how to describe it, yet I had felt it before. *I need this feeling and only this one with you. Why do I feel this way, angel? How do I feel this way?* The long hair they had was pushed back from their face. The inches away became less and less as they came even closer and suddenly their forehead rested against mine with their eyes closed. "Malach, I cannot wait to be free with you. You are the only thing I want to feel within this burden of an existence.

Just you." Their eyes opened and stared directly into mine. "Be free with me."

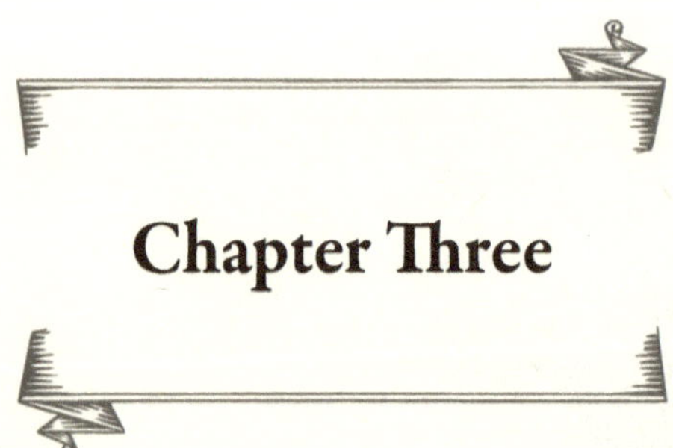

Chapter Three

I awoke from the dream floating in the middle of heaven. My body was still turned toward the angels shaping the cloud puffs. *Why does this sin keep doing this to me? I just said goodbye to Jophiel as well so I must wait to tell them. The angel said free again and that feeling. What is that feeling? I do not want to say it, but I almost like it. It was safe and calming yet something else that I cannot describe. How I wish to be able to find a word for it. Their eyes connected with mine at that moment. A connection...*

I shook my head at the thought of having a connection with another angel. Many things are forbidden in heaven, and I knew that I would not break those binding laws. I needed to continue on my way to my bible reading. While floating past the angels shaping the white puffs, I noticed that the clouds shimmered in color. It was a light blue that shimmered if an angel looked in the right spot. The shadow of angels illuminated that color as they floated quickly across it. *Another beauty that I seem to notice in heaven. How strange it is. It is almost as if heaven is not pure.* I shook my head. *What am I thinking? Heaven is pure and if they are a part of heaven then they are meant to be there.*

I arrived at my designated cloud. The bible reading area was designed in a corner of heaven where the sounds from above were not audible. It allowed us a moment to focus on our reading until our desired end of the event. One knew when it was the end of the event, yet it is never explained as to how we angels know. We just do. In these spots, our bibles lay on the cloud waiting for us to open them. I grabbed it and started moving the cloud around into the shape of a stand. It felt soft in my hands and almost nonexistent, but nonetheless, it shaped the way my hand moved around it. The light blue tint shimmered through each time I touched the cloud. My stand had a nice rounded base with an almost like a podium in a church which held my bible. Everything was smooth about the stand and everyone felt that it was almost as pure as they were in a sense.

My reading time was starting even if I was late, but I flipped through the pages looking for a chapter about sin. *Why would I continue to see acts of sin? This is worth my reading time to find out. Romans should say something about sin.* Romans 3:23 states, "For all have sinned and **fall short** of the glory of God." *I am pure so I shall not fall short. This did not help my understanding. I shall look again! Maybe in First John, it will say something!* 1 John 5:17 states, "All wrongdoing is sin, but there is sin that does not lead to **death**." *Could I die? I am eternal so I must not. Why does some sin not lead to death? Is that the kind of sin I am experiencing? Do angels experience sin? Does God trust us to not experience sin? No free will, right?*

I flipped to Job in hopes of reading something that would answer my questions. I stopped at Job 4:18 which says, "He puts no trust even in his servants; and against his angels he charges **error**." *Error? Does that mean like punish? There has only ever been one angel punished and that was Lucifer. No one knows where they went, but they were trusted and suddenly left. Now they are known as the Devil or Satan and one that commands sin! What does it say of Lucifer in the bible?* I flipped to Luke 10:18 which said, "And he said to them, 'I was watching Satan **fall** from heaven like lightning." *Fall? Did they fall? Like to the ground? A human will fall on the ground and hurt themselves, but angels float. Fall?*

I looked up from my bible after pondering the idea of falling. I shook my head at the thought and knew something was not right. Yet the bible said everything and of course, the bible was law. My eyes suddenly went black and then I saw the usual blinding light as I entered the dream. I was at another reading spot. It was not mine and the stand was shaped differently since it was not as smooth. The base was rough around with some permanent lines to imitate scratches. It had been used a lot and almost seemed ancient. At the top was a podium seen in a church, but the bible was worn and torn. It was flipped to the same page and passage as mine but had a black underline under the word fall as if it had some significance. *Whose spot is this? Why is it so torn and looks older? All of the spots are so neat and clean, but this one is not.*

I continued to look around and saw that the spot was lower in heaven to show that it was one of the first ones shaped by the clouds. There were words that almost looked like they were shaped permanently into the cloud. On one side it read "freedom" while the other said "burden." *These were similar words that had appeared in my visions before, but never one without the angel.* I felt tense in the area and almost unwanted. It was almost as if I should not be here. I floated out of the spot and looked up and suddenly there was a blinding light. I awoke in the spot I had been in before. *This was a particular spot in heaven like in the above! If they were lower than me could I go there and see?* I left my bible on the podium, floated out of my spot, and looked down. Many of the spots where other angels read went way down so I floated in the direction toward that spot. Somehow my body knew where it was and I could not tell why. I passed other spots with some wiser high angels who looked at me strangely. No low angel ever went down this far, but it was not forbidden. The lower you are, the longer you have been in heaven which meant that whoever's spot it was must have been here a long time.

While flying I started to ponder over the dreams I have had. *That angel made me feel safe, calm, and something else I cannot describe. Why are these dreams happening now and why would that angel want to be free? Free from heaven? That spot looked worn and torn. It was troubling to me, but almost like my troubled mind. I know I have to say it. There is a connection to that angel. I had a connection once or still do. Why do I not remember?* I stopped my troubled mind and somehow knew I was close to the reading area.

I looked to the left and saw the reading area. I floated inside and somehow everything from my dream was there, but the words carved into the clouds were no longer there. The bible sat in the same spot but was closed and showed the torn cover of the book and it was also on the same worn stand from my dream. My troubled mind could not understand this. Slowly and calmly I floated toward the bible and touched it gently. It felt different than mine with a rough edge. All our bibles were meant to be smooth, but this one was not. The bibles were black, which was another one of the only colors seen in heaven, with the words "Holy Bible" on the front. *Why is it so rough? Smoothness means purity, but everything in here is not smooth. What does the roughness of this area mean and whose spot was this?*

I opened it up and saw that many different things were underlined. Many different words. Normally in our bibles, they are clean and neat to show we are pure like the smoothness of everything in the area. Free was underlined in Galatians 5:1 as it said, "It is for freedom that Christ has set us <u>free</u>." *Whoever this area belongs to they sure like the idea of freedom. The angel from my visions also liked the same idea. Are they the same person? Like them, I wish to be free sometimes too.*

I closed the bible and decided to take it with me since the person who was there had not been there in a long moment. I flew back up toward my area to be able to hide the bible. Once I got there I noticed something was off about my area. I knew I had left my bible on the podium, but suddenly it was on the cloud in the spot where it was meant to be. *Was someone in my area? Did they see the page I left it on? What angel would do something like this?* I took the bible I had in my hand and put it inside the cloud to hide it. No one needed to know that I had another angel's bible, especially if it was connected to sin. I covered the hole in the cloud with some of the leftover puff and packed it in tight. Suddenly I heard the flapping of wings near the entrance, since it was so quiet, and looked over. Someone was there, but before I could say something my eyes went dark and I saw the light again.

I was standing in the spot I had previously been in after my last dream. A voice suddenly spoke. "Malach? What are you doing here?" I turned around and saw it was the angel from my previous dreams.

Somehow, I could finally speak to them. "I am sorry, but I wanted to see you again." *I did not mean to say that, but my body is saying it for me. Did this already happen? Am I remembering things?*

The angel shook their head and floated toward me. They did not wear a toga like the rest of us, but had a long cloak on that only wise angels wore. It was an ancient type of clothing that connected with the ancient-looking area. "You know we must be careful where we meet. No one can know about us." *No one can know? Who are they talking about?*

My body nodded my head for me in response. "I know, but you seemed uneasy the last moment we saw each other. I wanted to make sure you were okay."

They floated over toward their podium and lightly touched their bible. It was on the same page I saw it on last. "I am not. This burden of mine is not something I want anymore. I cannot tell you anything without fear of losing you." They turned and looked at me with a weary look in their eye. It was sincere and suddenly I saw a small shimmer in their eyes. The pin that was previously white had changed to the color black. *I knew it had changed colors previously! Why is it now black?* My body moved toward theirs and I was holding them in my arms. "I just want it to end. I need to fall." They said. *Fall? There is that word again. Did they want to fall? What does it mean?*

I held onto them tight as their head rested upon my shoulder with their arms wrapped around my waist. I felt something other than the angel on my shoulder. *What is that? It is... wet? They were crying. No angel ever cries to another.* My body moved my hand up to their hair and stroked it lightly in a calming way. "It is okay. We will fall together when we find out how." *Fall together? I wanted to fall. Why?*

They moved their head up to look at me and had a sad smile on their face. Suddenly my body started to feel a cosmic emotion that I still did not understand. It was like before, but it was radiating out of me faster than I could control it. My body smiled at them and moved my hand toward their cheek. I noticed they had the same marking as I did on my cheek which my thumb rubbed over as they smiled. My hand wiped away some of the tears that were running down their cheek.

Their face moved closer and rested on my forehead again like in the cloud-gazing dream. My hands wrapped themselves around their neck. This emotion was taking over my body and suddenly I knew what I wanted. *I want you and only you.* I finally knew that we did have a connection. It was becoming stronger and even more present between the angel and me. Suddenly a thought, like before, was being projected into my head. "Malach, I want you." Their hand moved from my hip to my face as they also caressed my cheek. Their thumb rubbed over that spot on my cheek that formed when I smiled like theirs. I felt their head lift from my forehead and move closer toward my lips. As they were moving another thought was projected into my head. They said, "You will be mine forever."

Chapter Four

A blinding light flashed through my eyes, and I noticed my hand was still on the cloud puff where the bible was packed in. *What kind of an angel would do that? There is a... I can say it... connection, but only in my mind. Is this connection still sin? Only high angels have connections so why do I have one too? Did my wish come true?* In my head, the words spoken by the angel repeated, "You will be mine forever." *I will be theirs forever? Maybe this connects to that cosmic emotion I felt.* I suddenly remembered that there was an angel at the entrance. I turned and looked, and Sariel was floating there.

They looked concerned and also upset like the angel did in my dream. *What happened to their human?* "Malach, I am sorry to interrupt your reading time and for having missed the daily meeting. I hope Jophiel was able to answer your questions that I could not." I nodded and Sariel floated inside the area and knelt down onto the cloud. They looked... *How to describe how they looked. It is like what I experienced with the angel. Tired?* The word was not spoken in the dream, but somehow, I knew and understood it fully. They looked tired and sad at this moment, but their pin still stayed white. *Why did the other angels turn black?* I shook my head to myself as I knew that this moment was not about me, but about helping my friend. I moved toward them and knelt down beside them.

"Sariel, there is no need to apologize. What happened with your human?" My hand moved to rub their back. Sariel also wore a toga-like the rest of us but had shoulder-length hair with as humans call bangs. It was straight as can be, but on their face, no dimple showed when they smiled so we shared a difference. Sariel moved their body and sat on the cloud with their knees close to their face. It was a cradle-like position that both of us knew seemed to calm the human emotions we felt, but Sariel more than myself.

"They lost it. They dreamed of wanting it so badly but lost it. My body hurts and so does my mind. This cosmic emotion hurts more than I want to believe. Malach, make it stop, please." Tears started rolling down their cheeks. They were clutching their stomach from the pain. Even though angels do not cry to another I knew that Sariel needed this. Angels have needs and wants too, but this was a need. It has never been forbidden to cry in front of another angel. *The angel in my dream knew that and even said they wanted me. Was this one of the needs and wants of angels?* I needed to focus on Sariel and not my own wants...

"She lost it. The cramping from her body hurt so much. She is safe, but it is gone. God allowed it to be lost. Why would they do such a thing?" Sariel looked up at me with tears streaming down their cheeks and their arm moved away from their stomach. I wrapped my arm that was rubbing their back around them to hold them close. Sariel leaned onto my body and just silently kept crying. This was the only way to get over a cosmic emotion. It needed to be let out and Sariel was doing that.

"It will be over soon. I am sorry your human lost the baby. I know their joy gave you the cosmic emotion too."

"She lost it and the joy I felt is gone. She will feel this pain for a long time. God took the baby away."

"They did because the baby was destined. You must remember that."

Sariel shook their head. "You are still very young, but God has done much worse than this. They do bad things and you must not trust them. Stay calm toward their Archangels and hide your true intentions." *Does God do bad things? How could they? Jophiel does not like Gabriel, but do they also not like God. The connected angel also does not like God. What is the truth?*

"What bad does God do?"

"They keep things from us. Things that should be known and we are trapped."

"Trapped?"

"Stuck in the same cycle every single moment. No escape for us. I do not want this burden anymore."

The words from the unknown angel repeated in my mind. "This burden of mine is not something I want anymore." I moved my arm away from Sariel and floated away from them. My back turned to face the cloud with the bible in it.

Sariel also floated up. "Malach? What is wrong?" There were dried tears on their cheeks and the cosmic emotion was starting to fade away.

"The angel said burden too."

"Angel? Who else thought this was a burden? What is their name?"

"I do not know. They appear only in those dreams. I never know when, but it has happened before."

"Have you told Jophiel?"

"Yes, but the dreams kept happening and I saw their area. They were here in heaven, and I had a..." I paused because if I said it aloud then it would be true. *Connection...*

"You two had a what Malach?" Sariel floated closer toward me. I could feel their presence only a few feet away. I took a deep breath to try to say it aloud again.

"We had a...con..," *I cannot say this aloud. I do not want it to be true as it would be almost committing to sin. Is this even sin?* I took another deep breath to finally say the rest of the word. "...connection." *It was true that we had a strong connection. Something cosmic that I had never felt before. They wanted to fall, which I am not sure what that means. Maybe it is like an escape.*

I slowly turned toward Sariel, having realized I finally said it until my eyes went dark. The light came again and an image started to focus. I noticed I was in the same position I was in the last dream. My arms were wrapped around their neck. Their hand was on my cheek rubbing that one spot and they moved closer toward my lips. I heard the thought projected into my head, "You will be mine forever." They were inches away from my lips when suddenly my body pulled back from theirs. *Why did I pull back? I remember this cosmic emotion and how much I wanted it and wished for it.* The emotion slowly faded away as my body floated there. The angel looked confused as they had dried tears on their cheeks.

"Malach, did I do something wrong?" Their face changed from a smile to a concerned look. They kept the distance that my body put between us.

"I know we have done this before, but I..." My body tensed up.

"Do you not like it? If I am doing something wrong tell me, please."

"I like it. I want it, but I am scared of being hurt." *Scared? What is scared? Wait! It means to be nervous. I am scared. Where did I learn this word? Did they teach me these words?*

"Malach, it is okay to be scared. I am too." They moved toward me and gently put my hands in theirs. "I would never hurt you, but if this is something you want then you can have it. You only have to ask, and I can show you the beauty of this or if you are not ready we can just stay here and talk."

I felt my body ease and I looked into their eyes. They were gray but they had a different thought in mind. I was not scared at this thought as somehow, I knew it was a desire to be held and wanted by them. *I want you too.* My body smiled at them and nodded. They pulled my arms that they held in their hands around their neck and put theirs on my waist. They held me close to their chest and suddenly I realized they were a bit taller than me, which was not unusual to see in heaven. Their bodily structure was of someone a bit active, and they stood straight and proud. I was so close that I could hear their heartbeat. "Thump, Thump, Thump" were the beats I heard from their chest.

We angels may not have souls, or at least we are told we do not, but we do have a heart like humans. It is how we can die. *I can die? How did I know this? The scripture was true which means I am not an eternal being.*

For the first moment, I noticed their wings. They were different than mine but had some scratches on them as if they had seen combat or rebelled. *They are almost as old as they look. Ancient like their spot and yet they chose me? Why?*

My body moved my face back from their chest and heartbeat. I looked up at them and smiled. I finally spoke. "We have a connection." They smiled at me and nodded.

Their finger moved over that dimple again which made my smile even larger. "We have a connection with this right here and..." Their hand moved toward my chest and put it on the spot where my heart was. "...here." Suddenly I pulled them toward me and put their lips on mine. The emotion started to pour out of me, and I knew I needed this more. *I want you and only you in this moment.* Their lips felt soft against mine and they were gentle with me.

They slowly pulled back from the kiss and smiled. In this moment they projected a thought into my mind. "You are mine. Let me have you here and now." My head nodded in response. They put their lips back on mine, but more aggressive this time. I knew they wanted me, and I wanted them. They moved from my mouth to my neck and were aggressive with their kisses. All while they were projecting thoughts into my head. "Malach, you belong to me in this moment. I can be yours forever if you let me." *I need to be theirs forever.* The sensation I felt was endless as they kept getting more and more aggressive. I could feel their hands start to dig into my shoulder underneath my toga. It felt like they were leaving a permanent mark on my body. Suddenly I heard another flapping of wings behind me, and the angel pulled away from me slowly. I turned and suddenly my eyes went black, and I was pushed back into the present moment.

Sariel floated in front of me with a very concerned look. I could not hear them, but I could tell they were talking. Returning from this dream was a bit different than before. I knew I had seen a longer vision. My vision of Sariel was blurred, and I could only hear silence around me.

Slowly, I closed my eyes and focused on how I was here in the present and not with the angel. My hearing slowly came back, and I heard Sariel again. "Malach? Malach? Light to Malach?" My head moved back and forth while I slowly opened my eyes. I could see Sariel perfectly now. "Are you okay?"

I slowly nodded and I realized I was not floating in the area but sitting on the cloud. "Sariel, how long was I gone?"

They looked with a worried look and said, "For a moment. A long moment. Your eyes went dark, and you slowly floated down to the cloud. I knew not what to do. Was this the dream you were talking about?" I nodded in response to them. I did not know how to explain it to them, but I tried.

After I caught them up, they finally understood what had just happened. "You mentioned they also said they were a burden. Do you know why?" I shook my head in response.

"They never mentioned why, but I do know that we had a very deep connection. It was almost like they were putting a permanent marking on my body." Suddenly I realized that if they had it would still be there and another piece of evidence that I was not wrong. I asked Sariel to look and they moved back my toga a bit in the spot and saw a little permanent line that was dug into my back. It was slight but it was there. *They truly made me theirs forever with this marking.* "They also mentioned this marking on my face was connected to them."

Sariel asked to see what the marking was, so I smiled and it appeared. They rubbed their hand gently over it to somehow get a feel for it, but nothing came to mind. Yet when they rubbed their hand over the marking it was gentle and calming. *Why so calming?* "We need to see Jophiel, Malach. They may know who this angel is or what it is about."

"Before we do that. I need to show you something." I slowly got up and uncovered the puff where the bible was. I handed it to them, and they opened it and started looking at all the underlined words. One of the words they saw was fall.

"Did you ever hear the word fall in your dreams."

"I did, but I am not sure what it means."

"There are rumors that we angels can fall from heaven. It is as I said, an escape from this burden. Was your connected angel trying to fall?"

"They were, but I also wanted to fall too." They nodded in response and somehow it was not shocking to them, but I did not understand why.

"We need to talk to Jophiel and ask them some questions and you need to keep having these dreams."

"Why?" I could not understand why they wanted me to have these dreams. *They did things to me physically if I continued to have them for long periods of moments. I will admit I am connected and that I want to continue having this cosmic emotion, but it is wrong.*

"This angel is the key to us falling."

"What if I do not want to anymore? Maybe I want to stay as pure as I am."

"If that is what you want, I am not going to force you, but let us talk to Jophiel anyway."

I nodded in agreement with this. Jophiel should know more about this and hopefully, they can make it stop. *This is not something I need anymore. I only want it. I wish for the dreams to stop.* Sariel nodded, but suddenly my vision of them went blurry and I saw the light again.

I was back where I was in the last dream. There was another angel behind me and the angel I had the connection with was looking at them. I turned and saw it was Jophiel. *Jophiel is here! They know! Did they lie earlier?* They crossed their arms and I saw their yellow pin start to flash another color. Yellow for them meant they could show us the beauty of humankind and bless it. The color started to turn into a mix of yellow and red. "Malach, we need to talk." My body tensed at the thought of them being mad. Their hair was shoulder length like the Sariel's, but they had a cold look in their eyes.

I noticed something behind Jophiel. In the distance, there was another angel that was floating and just watching. I could not make them out, but they turned away from what they saw. *Who is this other angel? Why are they spying on us from a distance? Why is Jophiel here with us and what the hell is this angel's name?*

Chapter Five

Sariel was shaking my shoulders to try to wake me up from my dream state again. There was silence around me and it almost felt peaceful. Returning from the dream state was a way to escape the thoughts of sin and the other angel. Slowly my eyes opened and I saw Sariel kneeling down beside me with their arms on my shoulders. Rather than looking concerned, they had an intrigued look as if they only wanted to know what I saw rather than seeing if I was okay. Sound engulfed my ears and I heard Sariel again.

"Malach, what happened?" I shook my head back and forth while I lifted my arms up to push them away slightly and to give myself some space. However, they did not stop talking. "I need to know. This is the key to us falling. What did they say or do this time? Were they kissing you again on the neck or did they move to..." I did not notice it a lot but my pin started to flash a different color. It was sort of a light pink. *Why is my pin flashing another color? This is all new.* Sariel continued on. "...your thigh or even project an image! Maybe they projected one of you two naked as humans starting to get closer and closer until..."

"Stop." Even though I interrupted them they did not stop.

"They get on top of you and start to tease you with their kisses like they did before. Making you feel this cosmic emotion that wants to burst out and..." Their hands were moving back and forth to continue explaining the point.

"Please stop." The light pink started to come through more on my pin.

"You end up bursting out and they touch that spot on your wing that makes you go crazy! They become aggressive again to put more markings on you and they say YOU ARE MIN..."

"SARIEL!" I shouted at them mid-sentence. They stopped and looked at me with a weird look that I could not describe, but I heard them gasp because they looked at my pin. I looked down and the light pink color had fully taken over the white that used to be there. *What happened to my pin? It is not meant to change colors! I know the angel's did in the dream but not mine... What is happening?* My breath was heavy at this moment and was rapid. I knew I was not calm.

Sariel flew closer and touched the pin gently and the color slowly went round and round in the pin. It was almost as if it would not be permanent but just for the moment. "What happened?"

I shook my head as I looked into their eyes. It was strange to see this different look on their face. *How to describe how they look. Is it... curious? They are looking at the pin with curiosity? They are because it is... interesting. I wish to continue learning these words.* "I am not sure why this is happening. The last time it happened was with the angel in my dream, but theirs turned black."

"Did they feel something cosmically?"

"Well, they were crying and... Wait! Do you think it turned black because they were sad?"

"I was just crying but mine stayed white. Maybe this was a different feeling. It could be something that not many angels feel, but you did."

"Why did I feel it, but not you?"

"This is why we need to talk to Jophiel and figure out these things."

I nodded my head and slowly started to calm my breathing which had gotten better while Sariel and I were talking. The light pink that was swirling around in my pin slowly started to fade each time I let out a breath. It was almost as if calming myself down helped the pin change color. Soon the light pink was gone and the white returned.

We floated out of my area toward the entrance to the above. Most angels do not go there when it is not the daily meeting but it is not forbidden. I could not understand why my pin would change colors. *Why does it change? I have seen this before but not like this.* Sariel interrupted my thoughts.

"I am sorry for not stopping. I did not think. How are you feeling about these dreams and the other angel?"

"Well, I am curious as to why these dreams are happening. I know the angel and I had a strong connection..."

"Very strong indeed." Sariel started to smile and laughed a bit to try to take away the seriousness of the conversation. I shook my head and smiled a bit.

"All of this is confusing and to be honest I say I want it to stop, but part of me does not." Images flashed through my mind of the angel and me during the last dream. Their long hair was pushed back just far enough for me to see their face. Their eyes were soft and gentle, but their lips were full and aggressive. It was a sort of balance that seemed nice to me in an almost pleasuring way. *Pleasuring? Did I just think this?* It was very slight but a little bit of color started to show again on my pin. This time it was a darker pink, but did not stay for long.

Sariel responded. "You think you need them to stop, but do not want them. It is your angel's needs and wants. What do you believe is the best course?"

"I think for purity they need to stop, but my heart..." I put my hand on my heart like the angel did when they spoke of our connection. "...does not want it to stop. It wants more." *I wish to be theirs forever. My heart wants them, but sometimes it feels it needs them.* I moved my hand slowly back down to my side and looked at Sariel. They smiled softly and I knew the true answer to their question. *I want these dreams to continue. They must.*

We finally arrived at the entrance and slowly floated up toward the above. The ring of light was not just white, but gold which showed the importance of it. It did not get very bright, but it was hard to see the little flicker every time an angel entered. Once we floated up inside the above we noticed Jophiel was already waiting for us. *This is strange. Normally they are not up in the above. We have to normally call for them to come. Something is not right.* Jophiel floated toward us with a smile on their face.

"Malach and Sariel I have been waiting for you. I had a feeling you two would want to talk about Malach's visions."

Sariel nodded. "We very much would like to. Malach has caught me up, but they have been happening more and more. We just want to understand."

I did not smile at Jophiel as I would normally have, but I did nod in agreement with Sariel. "Yes. I need to know why they are happening. They seem like sin but are not. I am confused."

Jophiel took a moment to look around the above to make sure no one was near. There was no one else in the above and so we knew we were safe. "Malach, tell me what you learned from these dreams."

I slowly nodded. "The angel was real. I saw their area with a bible. The area was ancient looking with words carved into the clouds. Their pin changed colors. Why do they do that? Also, they mentioned falling. What is falling? Can we as angels fall?"

Jophiel did not look surprised at these questions. *Have I asked these before? Do I not remember?* "I shall answer one question at a time. Yes, the pins can change colors. God forbids angels to know, as Gabriel says, to keep order. To explain the rest of the questions let me tell you a little forbidden history of heaven."

Jophiel started to move his hands as if to emphasize his storytelling skills. "A long time ago in heaven, angels used to live freely. Freedom was not forbidden and there was no hierarchy. Gabriel would say that there was no order then. Colors shined everywhere in heaven. Pins would change to beautiful colors that are now only seen on Earth. They displayed the emotions of angels, but they were not cosmic emotions.

They felt like humans did on Earth. No one felt as though they were superior to another. It was as I remember peaceful. Angels could feel like humans and almost be them, but little did they know they could. Falling. We learned that to fall we only needed to commit a sin. It could be anything but now angels could make a choice to either stay in heaven for eternal life or fall. Many angels fell to become humans, but there was still no order in heaven. Since many angels fell there was little left here so God stopped it. They created order and new angels. So freedom became forbidden, pins were now white, and falling was only just a rumor."

I was shocked! *Falling was known throughout heaven? Pins changed colors? What did I feel to make my pin turn light pink? The angel in my dreams was sad and theirs changed to black. Why?* Sariel was also trying to process what they just heard. They had a question. "Why did God change it and how did the new angels get created?"

Jophiel nodded and had a cold look on their face. "It was changed because there was little entertainment in heaven. Also, we became too much like humans. As for the new angels, God took the souls of humans and turned them into angels to help create the new order. Souls were as they say recycled to be used for God's wishes. They forgot their life on Earth, their loved ones, and the beauty of human life altogether. Souls could join others in heaven, but as you see now that is forbidden to help keep order. However, each soul that was recycled was left with a mark. It was on their face, but most hide it." Jophiel's pin started to show a hint of red as they finished speaking, but it slowly went away.

Sariel had a concerned look, and I could not process what I just heard. *I have a marking on my face. I hide it because it is different. Was I a human once and recycled for the purpose of God? Is this why the angel wanted to fall? Wait! I should ask why Jophiel was in my dreams.*

I looked up at Jophiel and they looked upset at what they just told us, but yet still calm. *How are they so calm?* "So God is bad? Does God lie to us? Gabriel does too?" They nodded. *God is bad. They are not pure.* "Was I a recycled soul?" Jophiel nodded again. "Why am I having these dreams and why were you in one of them?"

They lightly smiled. "It did work." I started to feel upset. Very lightly in my pin was the color red starting to show through.

I started to speak again. "What worked? Why is this happening?" Their smile got even bigger and small tears started to form in their eyes. *Why are they having tears?* The red started to show more through my pin. I could feel my heart start to race in my chest. Sariel was looking back and forth between Jophiel and me.

"It really did work. I am impressed and filled with joy." Jophiel had a huge smile on their face and the tears were getting bigger. My heart started to beat faster and faster. The pin filled with the color red.

"Tell me WHY!" Jophiel started to laugh and put their hand on my shoulder, but no tears fell from their face. *Are they hiding something?*

"It worked. Malach, you are having memories of an angel from the past." *Memories? So all of this did happen before.* Sariel's mouth opened wide and they were stunned at what we just heard. They had no words. *What did Jophiel do?* Suddenly my eyes went dark and light slowly peered through them and an image came into focus.

I was in the above and noticed many angels were leaving. The daily meeting had just ended and I was staring at the way the angels were leaving. I noticed the light blue particles that were coming up from them each time they floated away. *Was this the first time I saw them?* I kept staring in amazement at them. Suddenly I was interrupted. "Beautiful is it not?" I turned to look and saw the angel.

My head nodded in their direction. "I just saw them. It is so small yet so beautiful. God does wonders with this." I smiled a little and the mark on my cheek appeared. I noticed the angel staring at it. The angel did not look particularly interested in talking about God, but in this memory, my body did not seem to notice. They stuck their hand out, but I did not know what it meant.

"It is just a handshake. Humans do this on Earth. If I may?" They pointed at my hand and I nodded. They gently touched it and I felt the emotion start to rise up in me. *There it is again. How can I describe this?* My hand slowly touched theirs. "Now you introduce yourself."

My head shook in agreement. "My name is Malach." I smiled very softly.

"Nice to meet you, Malach." The hand moved up and down in unison with mine and I felt the emotion getting stronger. "My name is Raziel."

Chapter Six

This time instead of seeing black with the usual light peering through it was just a blinding light that continued onto the next memory. I could not understand it as it was almost as if I was going to remember everything about Raziel. *Their name is Raziel. So beautiful.* The blinding light slowly faded as another memory started to begin in front of me. It was the beginning of a new cycle in the above and I noticed Raziel talking to Jophiel. Both of them looked upset in some way but I did not know as to why. Jophiel moved quickly away from Raziel and I was about to turn to leave when they saw me floating there. They made their way toward me.

"Hey Malach!" *Hey? What kind of a word is this?* They could tell that I was confused as I did not understand.

"Hey? What does that mean?"

"I forgot you do not know a lot about humans. It is a way of greeting each other. Hello is also another greeting."

"Like the handshake?"

"Sort of, but it is different. Just trust me." They smiled and yet somehow as they said that I did trust them in a way. Not as much as I seemed to trust God at this point. *So, this memory must have been not long after we met. What is so important about this one?* "I wanted to see if you would join me in floating around a bit. I could teach you things about humans if you are interested?" My mind clearly was not understanding them at all. Maybe this is how it became "troubled."

"Interested?" Their smile faded a bit into a disappointed look. I could tell because their eyebrows scrunched up as if they were trying to think of a way to explain this.

"Just come with me and trust me. I will explain." They held out their hand as if to signal me to follow. Somehow, I was willing to take their hand and move along with them. *Maybe I was a little too trusting, but they did teach me new words.* The blinding light flashed through my eyes again, but different words started to "appear" in my mind. Words like consequence, pain, suffering, positivity, freeing, and interesting started to make sense. *I am not as troubled as I believe I am. Everything is new so I must learn.*

Another memory started to appear but this time we were by the gate of heaven. I knew I must have known them for a while at this point as I was starting to understand their words and "human" speak as I seemed to recall in the memory. Raziel floated in front of me with a despairing look. "Each soul that enters has no idea of what horror they are coming to."

This must have been my first encounter with God being not as pure since my body tensed. "What horror? God allows them to enter heaven for their eternal life. They will not be as pure as we are but can live a life of happiness. I would want that." Raziel turned around to face me and shook their head.

"This is not something that the souls want. I should know. I can feel…" They stopped mid-sentence and suddenly changed the subject. "Maybe you are right. Purity is essential." I could tell that I was saddened by their response. I felt "guilty" for saying we needed to be pure. *I understand the word guilty. Raziel felt something more than I could ever describe and I feel their pain. I wish for them to share that pain with me.*

Pain seemed to be a constant theme in these memories. *They were in pain and so they did something to take it away, but how did we get so close?* Light came through my eyes, and I started to see the image of my bible reading area. I was turned to a page on purity like I normally was, but Raziel floated into my area interrupting me. "Hey. Can I interrupt you for a moment?" I nodded and they continued. "Have you ever thought about being free?"

I shook my head and was appalled at their question. "How could you mention that here? Someone might hear you?" I floated closer toward them. "Freedom is forbidden." They nodded and seemed upset by my answer.

"I am sorry. I thought I would ask." They started to float away until suddenly without even a thought, I grabbed their hand gently. It was acting as a way to comfort them. Slowly a small smile appeared on their face as they were glad that I wanted them to stay. This was the first time I noticed it even though they had smiled many times before. They had the same marking I did on my cheek. *How beautiful you are. The pain you feel is endless. Let me take it away even for just a moment.* I pulled them back toward me and took their other hand in mine.

"Whatever you are feeling I want you to know that I am here. I am your friend. Talk to me or allow me to comfort you. Let me inside that heart of yours." I saw a small tear roll down their cheek and I took one hand off theirs to wipe it away. Their free hand gently pressed my hand against their cheek. The cosmic emotion started to arise in me again. I still could not describe it, but I knew something was different. *I need this forever.*

They softly spoke. "Thank you."

I nodded and the feeling slowly faded away as another image was being presented in my eyes through the blinding light. *That was the first time I caressed their cheek. Words are flooding into my mind every moment. I am feeling human.* I could tell that my feelings toward God and even Raziel were changing. During this time, I was thinking of freedom and being with them.

I started to recognize this memory. We were in the above during a daily meeting and Gabriel was speaking. Raziel was staring at me projecting thoughts into my head. Instead of focusing on them, I turned my attention to Gabriel. They were staring at Raziel, and me. Something is wrong here. *Do they know?* My attention on Gabriel was interrupted when the thought projected by Raziel popped into my head "Join me, won't you?" Our connection was getting stronger. Gabriel had finished speaking and before I could even move toward Raziel Gabriel appeared in front of me.

"Malach! How are you? How is your purity growing? Keeping an order of things?" I nodded at them in acceptance. *They know something is different.*

"Yes, Gabriel. I am growing my purity in the purest of ways. Everything is always in order as God allows." They nodded. I could tell Raziel was keeping their distance for important reasons. *Gabriel cannot find out.*

"That is good to hear. If there is any sin or word of freedom in your mind, I hope you know we Archangels are trained by God above to handle such things. You can always come to us, and we shall help you." Gabriel has said this to me before in the present. I could tell now how I recognized they were lying. They looked back and forth and had the same cold look. I nodded and soon Gabriel moved away from me. Raziel quickly floated toward me.

"Are you okay?" This was sweet. *Sweet is another word they taught me.* They cared for my well-being as I did them. I nodded and we quickly floated toward the entrance to the below. Jophiel quickly caught up with us though.

"Raziel. I need to speak with you." Both of us turned to face them and Jophiel realized I was also present. "Oh, Malach I did not know you knew Raziel. I hope they have been very nice." I nodded and was interested in seeing why Jophiel needed to talk to Raziel.

Raziel spoke. "Jophiel can this wait?" They looked a little upset, but I could not understand why. I did not like to see Raziel upset, especially not when it concerned another angel. *They are mine.* Jophiel shook their head. Raziel looked at me and softly touched my hand. "I will meet you there. It will not be more than a moment." There was a different emotion that started to rise in me. *Jealousy. Something nasty that looks like the color green I was told.* While Raziel was floating away they projected a thought in my head. "Do not worry. I am still yours." I smiled lightly at this. Light blinded my eyes and I knew a moment was passing by but it was not a long one.

I was floating in a spot in heaven where not many angels adventured to. *Adventure. It makes me think of the humans climbing mountains and traveling! I wish to travel and climb Mt. Everest one day! Maybe I will fall one day and get to.* I was looking at the clouds and realized that this was where Raziel and I cloud gazed. I felt a little tingling sensation around my body that I could not describe, but I knew I was excited. Raziel finally showed up and waved their hand.

"Malach, come imagine what these clouds look like." When I floated next to them our shoulders were touching. They started to point out the snake, but all I could focus on was how close we were. *I want to kiss them again. Feel their body pressed against mine.* Our wings slightly touched which caused Raziel to turn toward me and then they pointed out the bird. I smiled lightly and felt that feeling again. It was stronger this time. *I need this feeling and only this one with you.*

We became closer and closer and they rested their forehead against mine with both our eyes closed. I focused on the feeling of their head against mine as our bodies became closer. Our wings touched again. Suddenly they moved their wing across the edge of mine. The feeling I was having got stronger. I felt a little tingling sensation from it. *Are they teasing me?* They spoke again. "Malach, I cannot wait to be free with you. You are the only thing I want to feel within this burden of an existence. Just you." Their eyes opened and stared directly into mine. "Be free with me." The last time I had this dream it ended here but it continued on.

My arms moved around their neck and I held them close. "I will be free with you and only you." I closed my eyes again and so did they. We just floated there holding each other. I could feel their wing move against the edge toward the middle of my wing. They slowly moved it back and forth in a caressing way. I have never had this done, but I could imagine that this was equivalent to caressing one's cheek though this was more intimate.

As we just held each other Raziel decided to project an image they had into my mind. I saw many different colors and it looked like I was on a field on Earth. The grass was a darker shade of green and the trees had bright colors of yellow and red. Raziel did not have wings and was wearing human clothes. They had a bright purple shirt on with some jeans and what I would presume are sneakers. They also had a darker-colored jacket on to bring out the bright colors. They still kept their long hair, but instead of it being white it was a lighter brown with just a hint of red. I looked down at my clothing and I had jeans with sneakers on as well, but my shirt had some weird stripes. Raziel spoke and said, "It is called a flannel. It is a particular style for fall." *Seasons on Earth must be so nice. I wish to experience them all!* I could tell we were in the same forms we were in heaven but just without the wings and our usual clothing.

I wondered what color hair Raziel imagined me with. "What color is my hair?"

They smiled at my curiosity. "I could picture you with darker blonde hair. It would be shaggy." Suddenly my hair was transforming into shaggy hair that I could touch and pull down. It was an interesting style choice, but I liked it. I pushed my hair back and forth with my hand. Raziel walked closer to me as I was playing with my hair. They put their hand on my cheek and the marking still remained on my face. *They love to play with it. I am a recycled soul after all, but if they have the same one then they are too.*

I smiled. "What does this marking mean?"

Their smile faded but they kept rubbing my mark. "You used to be human. God made you into an angel to help the new order. They call us recycled souls." Raziel pulled me close to them.

"So, if I am a recycled soul, does this mean you are too?" I looked up to see their eyes and saw that they were not grey but a shade of green. Tears were forming in their eyes. They nodded but I could tell there was more to the story.

"I was the first. I cannot tell you much, but I can say that God made me the first. I saw them in their true form. I am not able to forget my time on Earth like the rest. My loved ones, friends, and experiences are still in my mind. I think about them every day. I may be a high angel, but I am stuck in heaven for eternity. That is part of my burden."

I wrapped my hands around their neck and pulled them into a hug. I could feel their tears landing on my shoulder as I just let them cry. *So much pain. Too much pain. God is not pure nor a good being. They are the true evil. Every angel needs to learn the truth.* I kept rubbing their back and we stayed in that spot for a while. The tears kept coming and I did not know how to make them stop. *I want to hear their whole story and take away that pain. How can I?*

Before I could even think of how I was able to stop their crying my body lifted their head off my shoulder and put both of my hands on their cheeks. Their complexion was red. The colors were so beautiful even when they were sad. *Raziel is so beautiful.* I put my forehead on theirs. "You are here with me and not in the past. God cannot hurt you here. Think about me and only me. I will help you." I saw a small smile form on their lips with the marking next to it. My hands pulled their face against mine and our lips gently touched. It was not for very long and we both pulled back slightly. It was our first kiss. My lips formed into a small smile and so did theirs. *This is what happiness looks like. Our connection looks like this. I like you Raziel and feel strongly about you.*

Another picture was presenting itself into my eyes where I was floating with Raziel in their reading area. I turned and saw Jophiel there with their arms crossed. "Malach, we need to talk." I saw the flash of red in the yellow of their pin. I remembered there was a figure who floated away in the distance and just as I remembered I saw them float away. *Were they the ones who entered my reading area in the present?*

I focused my attention back on Jophiel. "What did I do wrong?"

Jophiel floated closer toward Raziel and me. "Raziel and I have been talking about you. I am urging them not to fall with you just yet, but they will not listen and now I see you both here kissing! I am all for becoming like humans but you two need to be more careful!"

Raziel finally spoke up. "Why should we be careful? God does not care. They have never cared. You know that as well as I do. Besides you will not tell me how to fall with Malach." This is what has been going on between the two and why I saw them arguing. Raziel has been trying to figure out how to fall and Jophiel will not tell them how to do it. *Did they ever fall?*

Jophiel shook their head. "Gabriel is going to find out if they have not already. Since you guys are so careful!" They threw their hands up in the air. "If they do find out they will go to God and then both of you will be in trouble!"

Raziel put their hand on their forehead. *They are frustrated and I feel bad for them.* "I want to fall with Malach. So do they. Will you please tell us how? We just want to be happy. I want to be happy again."

Jophiel sighed. "Does Malach know the whole truth about you and why you were recycled?" Raziel shook their head. "You need to tell them and once you do that then I will tell you."

Raziel looked very upset. "If I do tell them then they could become a target!" *Target? What could happen?* Their pin was becoming a mixture of red and black. *Two emotions at once.* "I cannot take that chance! I love THEM!" The pin turned into a mixture of red, black, and a darker pink swirling around the pin. *Love? Love me?*

I gasped a little at what they just said. Jophiel looked between Raziel and me. "Tell them the truth and then we will talk." Jophiel turned and floated out of the reading area. Raziel had just realized what they said and looked horrified.

I turned toward them and put out my hand for comfort. "Let us talk about this. You can trust and tell me anything." Raziel shook their head.

"No, I cannot. I trust you, but I want to protect you." A small glimmer of tears showed in their eyes as they quickly floated away and I was left in the reading area. *They left me just like that.* I floated there alone in their reading area.

Slowly my body floated down onto the cloud where I knelt while the tears started to roll down my cheeks. All I felt was a pain in my heart. Everything around me was so silent to the point where I heard my own heartbeat. "Thump, Thump, Thump..." My hands covered my face as the tears rolled even faster. *I can handle this. I wish they would tell me.* I could tell that even while I was crying my marking started to show. *Are we really connected? Our connection was love? Yet they left me here and now. Will I ever see you again?*

Chapter Seven

Several memories started to play forth through my mind instead of the normal blinding light that would peer through. One of the memories was of me trying to find Raziel a few cycles later. They had just disappeared, and I did not see them. *Where did they go?* I checked everywhere but finally gave up. The next few memories were of me just going through the daily routine in a cycle, but all I could think about was them. Frequently I visited our spot where we cloud-gazed and first kissed. I would float onto a cloud and cry everything out until I remembered why I needed them. *I cannot have any doubts that you will not return. I need you in this eternal life.* While they were gone, I also did not see Jophiel at all. *Maybe they are together, but I wish they would return soon. I hope I am still theirs.* From time to time I wondered about this and a little bit of green would show in my pin, but it changed to black very quickly. Finally, the memories faded, and I was left with one single memory that started to play out in front of me.

I was floating in our spot like I normally did. I could not stop thinking about them so I did not go to the daily meeting and came here. I knew no other angel would be here since most listened to God and the above. Tears were forming in my eyes, and I could tell that my pin was black. I was looking at the clouds and trying to picture all those animals that Raziel was talking about until I suddenly heard a voice behind me.

"Beautiful is it not?" I knew that voice and turned and saw Raziel floating there with tears in their eyes as well. I could not even think before I rushed toward them and pulled them into a tight embrace.

"You did not leave me." I was crying harder and harder into their shoulder. "I missed you. All I could think about was you." *They came back for me.* They slowly pulled me back and put their hand on my face. Tears were still falling from their face. I could tell they looked different. The long hair they had was cut short to their shoulders. I missed the long flowing hair, but they looked beautiful no matter what they chose.

"I missed you too. My time was spent thinking of you and my story. I can tell you it to you, but you could be targeted or in other words hurt. I was forbidden to ever tell anyone. Not even the one I so desperately love." My heart started to beat faster and all I could do was nod my head as the tears kept streaming down my cheeks. *They do love me. I will take away any pain you have endured.* During that time alone I was able to understand what the word love meant. It was different from God's love and was more intimate. *Do I love them too?* They led me to a little cloud area that was near our spot, but on the way I kept my hand interlocked with theirs. I would not be letting them go again.

We made it to the area and shaped ourselves some seats to sit on and look at one another. "Are you sure you want to know? You could get hurt." I nodded my head.

"I do not care as long as I can keep you forever." They smiled softly and took my hand and held it gently.

"Before I entered heaven I went by a different name. People called me Cain."

I gasped a little. Cain and Abel was a story in the bible. It is told in the bible that Cain and Abel were the sons born to Adam and Eve, but that Cain killed his younger brother. "I know the story from the bible, but what is your side?"

My hands squeezed theirs a little more as they shifted a bit in the seat. I knew they did not want to tell their version of it but they did anyway. "The story goes as it says in the bible. I was the firstborn of Adam and Eve. Everything to them was always about God versus life because there was no one else to worship and if you did not then you would be sent to hell which was all we knew. You either chose to listen to God or you went to heaven. However, during that point, I also looked up to God. Then my little brother Abel was born. We never seemed to get along and had our own work to do. Since we loved God so much, we brought them gifts or sometimes sacrifices. I was a farmer and so I brought them crops. It was hard work, but my brother brought sheep as he was a herder. God seemed to favor Abels' gifts. I was so enraged, and it was something I had never felt before. I was the bad guy, and I will admit that killing someone is wrong. I regret every second of having killed my brother. Well, the bible goes on to say I was shunned and had to live out my days, but in truth, God did something that I probably deserved. After I died, instead of going to hell with Satan, I was brought to God themselves. They made me an angel, but I was left with a horrible burden..."

They shifted again. I was a little stunned at hearing that the person who loved me was none other than Cain, but after living through this torture for many cycles I wondered if they had learned anything. *Even though you were Cain somehow, I still want to take your pain away.*

They continued with the story. "My burden in heaven is that I have to remember my time on Earth, but also know everything that happened and will continue to happen to the humans. It may not sound bad, but I have to feel the pain of thousands dying every moment. I have learned to numb the pain and take it in, but in the process, I have lost myself. It was God's way of punishing me for murdering my brother. It is my eternal burden. I also have to relive my brother's death every cycle. God thought it would make me pure, but I have only gone crazy ever since. I am not pure but neither is God. After they realized they could turn me into an angel they started doing it with many others for the new order. Many souls did not realize what was happening until they saw that mark appear and then their memories were lost. Some realized it and screamed throughout heaven to plead with God, but it was no use. They forgot and lived in purity."

Tears started to roll faster down their cheeks. My hand squeezed theirs even harder. "You have been through this pain for many cycles. This does not change how I feel. I believe you are good and that you can be redeemed. I still want to fall with you and help you escape this burden and God." I smiled and we both got off the seats and hugged each other. Their head fit perfectly on my shoulder, and I just wanted to keep them there forever. "Raziel you are good. You have a past, but you have been redeemed in my eyes. I want to go home with you." *We are both recycled souls. I can take that pain away as you have to me. Let me be your home even for just a moment.*

I rubbed their hair ever so gently and they lifted their head slightly. Their full lips touched mine. I pulled back slightly and I could tell from their eyes that this was the moment we had wanted. Silently nodding they put their lips back on mine. Neither one of us knew what we were doing, but I knew that Raziel was going to take the lead.

Aggressively they pulled my waist against theirs squeezing it ever so slightly. Each of their kisses got longer and harder until they moved to my neck. That hand that laid ever so slightly on my waist moved to my thigh under my clothing. Keeping that gentle yet aggressive nature they moved the hand back and forth on that thigh letting me savor every touch while my hands wrapped around their neck. Raziel was allowed to take control over every single inch of my body. *Let this cosmic emotion take over me.*

Every touch I savored especially when they moved those lips from my neck to my ear. Using their ability, a thought popped into my head. "You are mine. I am going to take you – now and forever." *Anything for you.* Those gentle hands squeezed harder, gripping my thigh with silent and threatening carnality. One of their wings moved up against mine, teasing at the lightly feathered edge. Tendrils of lust built slowly from the pit of my stomach and prickled up my spine; the emotion inside me getting stronger with each stroke.

Colors flowed over my eyes and I saw an image come into focus. We were in that same field but with a small blanket over the grass. Raziel's body was on top of mine. There was pressure up against my body as they pushed me harder and harder to the ground. I was learning as I grabbed their waist and maneuvered them around so then I was on top. Slowly and ever so carefully I started to unbutton the flannel I was wearing while Raziel smiled. I got slower and slower, but each time their smile faded until they got impatient and pulled it apart. Brown-colored buttons flew off the flannel as they became more aggressive than they were previously.

Their hand moved from my waist to my neck as they pulled my lips down to theirs. Each sensation of their lips upon my mine enraptured me. A small moan escaped their mouth which was all new to me, but I relished this new experience. With one free hand, they stroked it around my behind going up and down. This was their revenge as it got slower and slower. The emotion inside me got stronger and stronger as theirs was too.

Suddenly they flipped me to the bottom as they decided they wanted more. Those hands that were upon me moved toward their own jacket as they ripped it off along with their shirt. Moving their way back onto me I took my hand and pushed them back as I slowly rubbed it across their chest to take a closer look at their body. Their chest was so smooth, but I could feel the bumps where the muscles were. Ever so carefully I moved my hand down to their waist. I motioned for them to move back and forth. They smiled and said, "Is this something you want Malach?" I nodded. That back-and-forth motion started to occur as I could feel the pressure of their thighs against mine. Both our emotions were getting stronger as I moved my other hand across their chest.

The pressure got harder and harder the more my hand moved across their chest. Faster and faster did they move and each time I wanted more. *I am never letting you go.* However, they suddenly stopped. *Another revenge tactic?* Those full lips pressed hard against mine. Each kiss I savored as they moved from my neck down to my chest. Little bite marks were left at every spot their lips touched on my body. Small pains lingered in each of those spots as they continued to nibble at my skin. They moved down my body and those pains became more aggressive, but the emotion I felt started to pour out of me. Raziel knew what they were doing and how to do it well.

Their kisses got closer toward my pants as they looked up and smiled. One hand moved over the button and carefully took off the pants. I could feel the pressure of them pulling them down. I heard a sigh as they knew it was taking too long. Instead of carefully pulling them down I felt a large pain on my thighs as they ripped them off. Underneath I was wearing nothing and those kisses resumed, but on my thighs. One pain lingered in a certain spot on my thigh and when they moved to look up at me I saw a dark purple marking. "Now you are truly mine." Those kisses moved from the left thigh over to the right, but they never left another marking like the one they did before.

As smooth as they could be they moved those full lips onto mine. My hands moved off their body down toward my pants as I wanted them to feel the same sensation I felt. *If I am yours then you shall be mine.* I remembered how they flipped me before and so slowly I was able to get on top. Mimicking the kisses I felt earlier, I slowly moved down on their body. My pleasure was in teasing them since they started to squirm whenever my kisses were too slow. Instead of leaving a mark on their thigh, I left one on their neck. Nibbling on their neck seemed to start the process as I heard another soft moan escape from their mouth. I bit a little harder and saw a small purple marking appear. With my hands on their waist, I squeezed them harder and harder each time I knew they would feel pain.

Slowly I moved back and forth with my waist as the pressure would get soft then harder as I pressed against theirs. Their emotion started to pour out of them. A small little bright light would shine from our body to tell us if we were pleased. My waist moved faster and faster and the pressure became harder and harder. The light started to get bigger and bigger out of both of us. A longer moan escaped from Raziel's mouth. My lips moved to their neck as I got more aggressive with each thrust of my body.

Raziel suddenly wanted control as the image went out of focus and we were back in heaven. Their hands were around my waist, and I stopped kissing their neck to notice where we were. Our clothing was off and there were small little scars on their body. Slowly and gently, I rubbed my hands over them, but they continued the aggression I started. My waist was pulled against theirs.

A cloud suddenly transformed into the shape of a table. The feeling of pressure against my back was present as they pushed me harder into it, kissing me in every single spot I wanted. As they continued kissing me, I was lifted on top of the table with my legs spread apart. Our bodies fit ever so perfectly while my legs wrapped around them. The light emitting from us got brighter and brighter. Back and forth went their waist as they were forceful with their thrusts. Our wings intertwined with one another, each rubbing those spots that pleased us both. One of Raziel's wings was rubbing mine in the middle as my wing rubbed at the edge of theirs harder and harder. Suddenly that light started to burst. It was so bright that it blinded both of our eyes. It was a big ball of light. *Our big finish.*

Raziel slowed and we both held each other close. Their head rested upon my chest. Our clothes were still off which gave me a moment to look closer at their scars. Some were on their chest, but bigger scars were laid upon their back. It almost looked like they drove their nails across those spots. These scars were long and dug into the skin. I gently moved my hand over one of them. They felt the same as they looked.

"I did that." I jumped a little once Raziel spoke. "You do not remember your transformation, but I remember mine. I could not tear off the wings and so God left me a permanent reminder of it." I could not help but keep rubbing my hand slowly over it. *I will remember every single pain you ever felt. God will get what they deserve.*

We did not know how many moments passed, but we just stayed in each other's arms. *I meant it when I said I would never let you go again.* Raziel slowly started to let me go, but I pulled them back against my body. "I am not letting you go." They laughed a bit as they stayed in the spot I wanted them to.

"You really are demanding." I grabbed their hair and pulled them lightly to look up at me.

"Only for you." I kissed them playfully and held them even closer.

Suddenly a flapping of wings was sounding from the distance. We quickly realized that the sound was getting closer and closer. Raziel picked up my toga and threw it at me as they quickly grabbed their long cloak to put it on. Somehow we were able to get dressed before Gabriel floated to us.

"Malach, I was wondering where you were. You were not at the daily meeting. Is something interrupting the purity in your heart? God was troubled when you did not show up." *God was worried? Are they lying?*

Raziel floated closer toward me as if to protect me from Gabriel. Raziel spoke. "I am sorry but that is my fault. I had a piece of scripture to show Malach to help grow their purity. We were just floating back towards the above to join everyone at the daily meeting."

Gabriel squinted their eyes as if to signal that they did not believe Raziel. "I see. What piece of scripture was it that you thought Malach needed to know right now?"

Raziel's face stayed ever so calm. *They are almost like Jophiel. Both of them stay so calm. How?* "It was Psalm 119:9 that states, 'How can a young man keep his way pure? By guarding it according to your word' because as you know Gabriel I always keep my word." I could tell they were smiling a bit as their mark started to show. *You can be so calm yet are so charming at the same time. I get to keep that.* My eyes wandered over their body as I could not stop staring and remembering the feeling of their body against mine. *How I wish to have you like that again.* A thought was projected into my mind. "I love you, but Gabriel might notice. I will take you again later my love." My eyes quickly shifted away from staring at them to looking back at Gabriel. I wish I could have smirked at that moment.

They looked between both of us and nodded. "That is a very pure passage in the bible and I am glad that you were able to show them." For the first time, I saw Gabriel smile a bit. *They must truly believe this.* "I shall leave you two, but please make it to the daily meeting. God would not want you two to miss. Especially Malach. They take notice of these things." Slowly they floated away.

Once we believed that Gabriel was a distance away, we both started to laugh. Our markings were showing, but it did not matter. I wrapped my arms around them and just held them close. "I am so happy to have you. I cannot wait to spend the rest of our lives on Earth."

Raziel pulled me in for a long passionate kiss. I could feel the feeling start to rise up in me. We broke apart for just enough time for them to say something. "Let me show you my love again." I put my lips back on theirs and the memory started to go out of focus. I remember that we did not leave that spot for many moments, but we did go to the next daily meeting to help keep the lie in place. I could not stop thinking about them. *All this happiness is so overwhelming. Why did I forget you? Did Jophiel ever tell us? What happened with God? Before I met you I only wished, but now that I know you I need to remember.*

Chapter Eight

"MALACH!" A voice screamed as it echoed throughout my ears. I opened my eyes slowly and saw the blinding light shine through my eyes, but soon a blurry image came into focus. *Who screamed?* White was blending together, but I saw two faces looking at me worried and I felt my shoulders being shaken back and forth. Everything was silent in my ears and somehow it was still that sense of peace that I enjoyed before. Nothing to worry about, but my vision starts to focus on the two faces. Jophiel is mouthing my name while shaking my shoulder, but Sariel is caressing my face to try to make sure I am okay. *They almost seem like a version of a mother at this moment. No wonder they were as excited as their human to have a child.* I start to hear the sound of Jophiel's voice come through my ears, but everything is very slow. My dream was longer this time, but there were multiple. *Raziel is their name, we met in the above, they taught me how to embrace humanity, and we felt something that was beyond a cosmic emotion. All of this was hidden from God, yet I still wonder where they went and how I forgot them.*

While my thoughts were racing the sound of Jophiel's voice was getting louder and louder in my ears. "Malach? Are you able to hear me?" I shook my head and Jophiel breathed a sigh of relief. Sariel was still rubbing their hand over my forehead to my cheek. They were concerned and the sensation of their hand was calming. *It reminds me of Raziel and how they moved their hand over my mark to calm me down.*

I looked around and I was in the above but I was on the top of the big cloud. I must have floated down toward it when the dreams started.

Slowly I started to move to get up and Sariel offered their hand to help me which I took. They said, "What happened?" The hand that was on my cheek was now on my shoulder trying to help keep me floating.

"Raziel happened." I smiled at being able to say their name finally. *I miss you.*

Sariel spoke. "Raziel? I do not recognize the name. Were they the angel you had a connection with?"

I nodded. "Our connection was strong. They loved me and I really cared for them. We were going to fall together and they taught me how to speak like a human. To embrace humanity as they said."

Jophiel was smiling at this. "I am glad it worked. Did you get the full story?" I shook my head and Sariel brought me in for a hug.

"I am glad you know. Your connection must have been pure." I moved back slightly from the hug.

"It was not pure. No angel nor God is pure. It was happiness. Pure happiness if you call it pure."

Sariel smiled and started to have tears in their eyes. "You finally now realize what I have been saying. It is a burden here. God takes away things most important to humans and angels. They took Raziel away from you right?"

"I do not know. I think so, but I am not sure where they went. All I remember is Gabriel almost finding Raziel and I after we..." I slightly did not know how to answer.

"After you?" Sariel cocked their head to the side with a look of confusion on their face.

"We might have..." I started to look embarrassed and saw my pin changing to a light pink color like I had seen before.

The tears had disappeared from their eyes and instead, they smirked. "Malach you two did not."

"We might have." Jophiel was beside us starting to laugh.

Sariel opened their mouth wide. They let go of me and playfully hit me on the shoulder. "You two did it like humans! No wonder you had such an intimate connection." They gave me a playful smirk. My hand went over my eyes, and I shook my head.

Jophiel was laughing hysterically and so did Sariel. *I may miss Raziel, but I am glad I have these two to help me. Happiness is here too with my friends.* We all started to calm down and Jophiel looked at me.

"What is the last thing you remember?"

"We had just fooled Gabriel."

Jophiel shook their head. "You do not have the full story. You know who Raziel was, but not what happened. You do not know the purpose of you keeping these memories."

I started to look concerned. "What is the purpose? Not just because they loved me? Jophiel what happened to Raziel?"

They crossed their arms. "I used my ability to store these memories. I do not control when they come back. You do it when you are ready. I made sure your love for them is not forgotten. Heaven needs you, Malach." I floated back a little. *Heaven needs me? I need to be ready? Do I love Raziel? I know I feel strongly about them, but I am not sure it is love.*

"Heaven needs me for what?"

Sariel chimed in. "There is a purpose for this. You have a destiny."

Sariel knows? I shook my head. "Destiny? Angels do not have that."

Jophiel shook their head. "That is another lie God told. You have a destiny. That is why heaven needs you. You need to be ready to remember those memories." *What can I do? I am just a low angel.*

"Why am I so special?" *I cannot be this special.*

"You devoted yourself to God while you were human and joined the other souls in heaven. You were turned into a recycled soul in order to lead the new order. Raziel may have been the first, but you were the 'prophet' for this new order. You were meant to show all of us that

God was good and that we should be pure. You were meant to be an Archangel that would be God's closest ally and above Gabriel."

My hand went over my mouth. *Me a prophet?* "I am not an Archangel! I am just like every other low angel."

Jophiel floated closer and put their hands on my shoulders. "You are the prophet of heaven. Gabriel found this out and made sure you would be a low angel. They stayed closest to God and made sure of this new order. Your destiny was to show us to be pure. You have learned this before with Raziel."

Instead of going into the normal dream state, I started to remember the memory that played inside my mind. *Is it still troubled?* Raziel and I were near the entrance to heaven, and I saw Gabriel floating next to us. "Malach how I have always despised you. God looked after you and only cared for you. Always you and never me. I have stayed closest to them. Now you want to go and defy God like this! Thank you Job for being the most devoted to God and yet betraying them like Judas!" *Job? Job? I was Job from the bible?*

Job was a man from the bible who gave up everything while believing in the lord. After slightly doubting God and losing everything God finally gave him everything of his back plus a little more. He stayed true to God until the end even after losing everything. I remember myself starting to speak. "You know why I have to go against them. God and you controlled everything. The new order was your idea this entire time. I cannot let you two control me or anyone else! None of this needs to happen again. I sacrificed everything for God as a human to just forget it all in heaven instead of the eternal paradise I was promised!" Gabriel started to float closer toward me. Raziel put their body in front of me to protect me.

Suddenly there was a loud voice echoing from above that stopped Gabriel from inching closer. All of our heads turned toward the entrance and saw a glowing light emitting. *God.* That is where my memory ended. *What happened after?*

The scene stopped playing in my mind and I looked up at Jophiel. "My name was Job and I made it to heaven after I died. Yet I forgot everything to become this prophet for their use. The new order is wrong. I am needed to help bring freedom to heaven. Everyone should be able to have the eternal paradise they were promised."

Jophiel and Sariel nodded in unison. *How am I supposed to unite heaven?* Jophiel spoke. "You remember. The memories may come back like they did before or you may just remember them. I cannot tell you, but can help trigger some."

Jophiel thought for a moment on how to help trigger the rest. I noticed that they were letting their pin freely change colors. It went from yellow to blue with a hint of orange. *Blue means they are in deep thought while orange is determination. I remember Raziel teaching me all the colors. This is like how Jophiel said it would happen.* Angels can control if their pins show the color if they are taught. Once you break the cycle of it always being white then you can learn to control it.

Jophiel finally spoke. "You need to remember where Raziel is and how you forgot. Then you will fully understand your prophecy. It was beautiful." *Their loss was beautiful?*

I was slightly annoyed by their phrasing. The color red started to show through my pin. "How was the loss of them beautiful?"

"Something happened that was beautiful. The loss of them triggered it. You found your prophecy. By remembering you will be able to unite all of heaven against God. Heaven is the only choice."

Heaven cannot be the only choice. Raziel is one too. What happened when I found out? My body starts to go into the normal dream state. The image starts to go into focus and I am in Raziel and my spot. Jophiel is there with Raziel and me. I had just been told I was Job from the bible and found out part of my destiny for Heaven.

Jophiel speaks. "Malach you are the prophet we need for freedom. You can fall after you help heaven."

Raziel butts into the conversation. "We want to be rid of this place and spend a human life together. How long will it take?" They grabbed my hand. I looked at them and could tell that I was smiling at them.

"Raziel is telling the truth. I want to spend my life with them on Earth. It cannot wait."

Jophiel shook their head. "We need to unlock your ability which is something I have never done. There is no time limit for this. Heaven is all that matters. Think of the freedom of all angels."

Raziel's hand gripped mine harder. They spoke. "I have spent an eternity feeling the deaths of thousands and living out my punishment. Malach is the only good thing to come from my time in heaven. I cannot stand being here longer than is needed. They are more important to me than heaven and its freedom. I love them."

Jophiel's pin started to turn a little red. "They are the only ones who can restore freedom to heaven. We need them. I am not going to give them up just because of love. I love heaven and it's angels. They have lives too."

Raziel and Jophiel started to inch closer to each other. By this time Raziel had let go of my hand and I was stuck in the middle of them arguing.

Raziel spoke. "I need them too. I will not survive my human life without them."

Jophiel was speaking over them. "Heaven needs its savior. It needs them."

"How can they save them all? God cannot be stopped!"

"Destiny can save them all!" *This is not good.*

"Heaven be damned. Malach do not listen to Jophiel!" *The pressure.*

"How dare you say that! Heaven is everything. Malach do not listen to Raziel!" *I feel like I am backed into a corner. This is something new to me that I have never felt before.*

In unison, they looked at me and said, "Choose me!"

By this time both of their pins were red, but mine was a different color. It was a mix of red for passion and orange for determination. *Both sides have a point.* I wanted to help them both, but I was told to pick one. *Raziel or Heaven. I can only pick one.*

I looked at Jophiel and saw the determination they had for liberating heaven, but then my eyes moved to Raziel. I could see the love for me they had in my eyes. *How can I choose?* The dream state started to end, but instead of focusing on another image I heard the scream again. "MALACH!" *Raziel?*

Chapter Nine

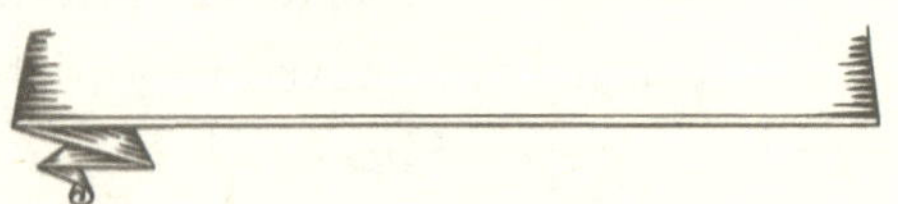

"Save me." Someone spoke. I moved my head back and forth to try to get out of the dream state I was in. When I opened my eyes, I did not see Sariel or Jophiel. Instead, there was a black void. The same unknown voice spoke yet it was so quiet as if it was a whisper. "Remember it all please."

I looked around. "How can I remember you if I do not know who you are?"

The voice was louder this time. "You know who I am. You know the good parts, but you need to finish my story." *Who is speaking? Raziel? Gabriel? God?*

"Tell me your name please," I said.

"I cannot. You know it."

"Did you scream?"

"Yes."

"Raziel is that you?"

"Yes, my love."

My body started to tremble. *I can speak to them? How?* "How can I speak to you?"

"Jophiel kept my memory alive enough for me to speak to you just as a memory. You need to remember everything. Start at the beginning."

I saw a blinding light, but I stayed in the black void just watching it happen in front of me instead of in the normal dream state.

Raziel was called Cain in this memory. Cain said, "How am I here? Why in heaven?" God was there in the abyss of their home. Light surrounded the home and it seemed to on forever. In the middle of this abyss was a circular shape with chairs surrounding the throne that sat in the middle. *Gods throne.* Gold covered the throne and the floor was raised in that spot to make God seem higher than others. The chairs were not like the clouds down in heaven. It was a strong metallic type like the throne, but each one was a different color. *Assigned seats?* On the floor was a gold Star of David. A huge ball of light filled with many different colors like the chairs started to float closer toward Cain. Those colors started to diminish the closer they got to him. I could only see the back of God.

"You shall be punished for all you did. Murdering is not the entertainment I need. My son enjoys it enough." God's light diminished till they were finally in an angel form. Their wings were large and filled with many different colors. *So much evil yet so beautiful.* Before they let Cain speak they raised their hand and he started to float above. They moved their hands in a certain way while Cain's body was twisting in all directions.

He screamed. "WHY! LET THIS AGONY END!"

God only laughed louder and louder. With every scream from Cain, God's voice got bigger and bigger. This was meant to show him who is the boss of him and the whole world. The wings started to morph from his back. The bones of his body were taken out and made into wings. Cain's hands moved to his back to try to stop and rip them off. God saw this and quickly made his nails longer as if they were claws that dug into the back. God said, "You will never forget your punishment or that you may never return to Earth. Remember and try to grow in my purity. This is your eternity in hell." They laughed after their statement.

Cain was groaning in pain until God froze their hands in place. Cain's body fell to the floor. He was in front of God's Throne as if he was bowing down to God. His body had changed into a full formed angel, but blood was spewing from his back where the wings were. The red was so bright against the golden star on the floor. A little laugh escaped God's mouth as they moved closer toward an unconscious Cain. They picked up one of Cain's arms to make sure every inch of them was perfect and pure. God spoke again, "You shall be known as Raziel. Never mention your old name. For those who know shall be hurt by my wrath. You will be pure in the purest of ways. Remember this." Even though Raziel was unconscious they knew and would remember for many cycles.

The bright light from the memory started to fade until I could only see the black void. *No wonder they hate God.* "God needed to be stopped. How did I forget all of this and you?"

Raziel's voice spoke. "You had a choice to make." *Heaven or Raziel.*

The light was starting to show through the black void and another memory was playing out. Jophiel and Raziel had both said to choose them. My instinct of knowing my destiny was to choose heaven, but my heart was pulling me toward Raziel. *Can heaven change without me?*

Both of them were looking at me and I was too stunned to speak. *Why does my destiny have to be this? I wish to do both.* I took a deep breath and grabbed Raziel's hand. "Jophiel I will help you if you tell Raziel how to fall." *They never told us how even after Raziel told me the truth about them.* My hand gripped harder on Raziel's. They knew what it meant if I chose heaven.

Jophiel took a moment before they answered. Their pin showed blue for the deep thought. Meanwhile, Raziel's was starting to turn slightly black. A thought was projected into my head. "How can I survive without you? I am meant to protect you." Tears started to form in my eyes. *They protected me this far, but if I could help heaven and protect everyone from God's wrath I would.*

Jophiel finally answered. "Fine. To fall you need to sin at the entrance of heaven. Angels have sinned in other spots of heaven, but you can only fall at the place where a human enters from. That is the way to return 'home.' Now that you know Malach we need to get started right away. Gabriel knows." Before I could even say a word Jophiel ripped me out of the grasp of Raziel and floated quickly away with me. *Gabriel knew? How? We lied and kept a secret.*

The memory started to fade and the black void was left in my presence. "How did I get to be with you when God spoke to us?"

Raziel said, "You need to remember, not me."

Their voice sounded stern at this moment. I said, "You are supposed to help me. If I protected you then why is heaven not free now? Why did I forget you? What went wrong?"

"You are asking the wrong questions. Think harder!" Raziel's memory was getting angry at all my questions.

My arms went up in the air. "How am I supposed to know? I forgot you! How can I trigger something I do not know."

"Feel Malach. Think like a human. You know how. Why did you do what you did?"

"Because I cared strongly for you! We had this connection! Somehow I needed to do both, but I could only do that if I protected you!"

"You are almost there. Why did you protect me?"

"I cared for you that's why!" I was starting to get upset with them for asking all the questions now. *Why else would I protect you?*

"Think deeper. What did you feel?"

"I felt passion for you. I knew even though after everything you did on Earth you deserved a second chance. That was supposed to be your life in heaven. Instead, you were punished. I felt the passion and determination that you had to be able to escape this place. That pain you shared with me. We connected and united in pain and passion. That feeling is more than I can describe." My hands had moved over my heart.

"Describe it."

Tears started to form in my eyes as the tension in the void got to be more and more. "I just told you that I cannot describe it! It felt more real than anything I had ever felt. I..."

"You what Malach? Why would you protect someone like me, give me a second chance, and want, after everything I told you, to still fall with me? WHY?"

The tears were rolling down my cheeks. I started to crumble onto the black ground. My hands moved to cover my face. I could not speak. *I miss you more than I can describe. I wish to have you back.*

Raziel's memory was getting more and more upset. "WHY MALACH? TELL ME WHY. I WAS MEANT TO PROTECT YOU!" My hands slowly started to clench into fists. Their voice seemed to surround me like it was never-ending. From the right I heard. "WHY AFTER EVERYTHING?" From the left I heard "TELL ME!" Every part of my body tensed up at every word they said. It was all too much.

With every bone in my body, I decided enough was enough. I quickly stood and said, "Because I LOVED YOU DAMMIT!" My voice echoed throughout the void. *I had never said it aloud till now. I only thought it because I was too scared for it to be true. Even after everything they have told me I was too scared to say it till now. It was like having a connection. I was too afraid to believe that any of this was true, but it was. I loved them more than I could describe. I would give up my life for theirs if it meant they could have a chance at escaping heaven.*

The memory I had wanted to see started to appear in front of me. My teary eyes looked into the light to see Gabriel, Raziel, and me at the entrance of heaven. I remembered that while I was with Jophiel figuring out how to unlock my ability I realized my feelings for Raziel. I knew that heaven would need me, but that my love for Raziel was too strong to at least not say goodbye. I quickly floated away from Jophiel and was able to catch up with Raziel at the entrance. For some reason, no angels were around, but I had just hugged them until Gabriel had shown. God had yelled at Gabriel to stand back.

All three of us looked toward the entrance to the above. There was a big ball of light that was floating down. *It is God. I remember their true form. I saw it in Raziel's transformation.* The light got closer and closer but all we could do was float in the same spots. Like many other subtle things in heaven, there were small little details on God's ball of light. Sparks of all colors were showing with every move they made. Little particles emitted from those sparks. *Such beauty in something so bad.* It got closer and closer toward us until finally, the light had started to fade away until God's true form was revealed. I had only seen them from the back. They were taller than all of us with pure white skin like the rest of us. Their hair was cut to their shoulders, but the wings on their back glowed with many different colors. *A rainbow.* They smiled at Raziel and me. A marking appeared on their cheek. *Are they recycled too? Or is the marking meant to signify that we are the work of God's creation?*

They spoke. "If it is not Raziel and Malach or should I say Cain and Job. You two have been bad angels. Strayed away from all the purity I have given you. Especially you Malach. You were meant to be the prophet to lead this new order. A shame you could not." My fists were clenched while Gabriel floated to stand next to God. *Some right-hand man.* Raziel was floating by my side. *We shall protect each other no matter what happens.*

I looked up at God. "My only destiny is to bring freedom to heaven. There is no such thing as purity." My hand grabbed Raziel's and squeezed it tight.

God laughed at us. "Such a united front you two are. No one can stop me."

Suddenly a voice was heard from behind Gabriel and God. "Malach can and will." God turned and saw Jophiel floating there.

"Jophiel. How wonderful for you to join us. You were saying?" I had not seen it before but there was a holster on the side of Jophiel's clothing. A sword was there. Glancing toward Gabriel I also saw a sword holstered to the side of their armor. *A battle?*

Jophiel drew their sword. It glowed yellow like their pin. Determination for the freedom of heaven while Gabriel drew theirs and it was blue with a bit of white which meant the protection of heaven and purity. *Wow. Each one is so beautiful yet one means good while the other is evil.*

God turned their attention back to us as Gabriel and Jophiel floated quickly toward each other. One protecting the fate of the other. When the swords touched there was a huge light of many different colors. *Two ideas collide.* While they were fighting God spoke to us. "Now I believe now is a good time to say goodbye. Both of you have had a good run. Let us erase those minds again shall we?" With one hand God lifted Raziel higher into the air. I could not reach them, but they started to groan in pain. "Cain you can get everything you have always wanted. To forget everything most dear and precious to your heart. All the love you had on Earth and even shared in heaven shall be gone forever."

God twisted their hand back and forth as Raziel groaned in more pain yet they still called out for my help. "Malach PLEASE!" *How can I do anything?*

I spoke. "Please make it stop. Take me instead. Leave them alone."

God looked directly into my eyes. "If they do not forget then it could start over again. Everything must be in order. I will have ORDER!" Their hand made a jabbing movement which made Raziel groan in more pain. *Stabbing them.*

"Please. Kill me or make me the prophet I am meant to be. Leave them." I begged God to let my love go.

God slowly put their hand down and lowered Raziel. "Someone so willing to forget everything to protect their lover. How human of you." They took their other hand and raised me up in the air. "I would be willing to accept this."

Raziel moaned in pain. "No. Malach do not. I beg you." My heart yearned for them. *I can only protect them like this.* God started to squeeze their fist and it felt like my body was breaking into many different pieces. My heart started to beat faster and faster. I looked off in the distance and saw Jophiel starting to lose the battle against Gabriel. *Everything is crumbling down.* Raziel had tears in their eyes. "God please do not do this. Let them go please."

Tears started to form in my eyes as I felt every bone in my body breaking. *I failed. Failed to save heaven and failed to fully protect my love.* Suddenly the fighting behind God had stopped. I looked over while in pain to see Jophiel had knocked Gabriel out and was running to save us.

God flicked their hand and I fell onto the cloud. They turned to face Jophiel just in time for them to swing their sword down. They were not able to move. Raziel rushed toward me in just as much pain while Jophiel was keeping the attention of God. Both of their hands cupped my face to hold me close. One rubbed my mark to calm me down while the other went across my hair. All I could focus on was being close to them and staying that way until a thought was projected into my mind. "We need to go now. Please come with me." I was still in a lot of pain but I managed to nod yes to them. A smile appeared on their face and they slowly lifted me up to carry me to where the souls entered from. *They have so much strength after God hurt them. Maybe they endured it as they have felt the pain of thousands dying for many cycles.* The entrance was in the shape the last soul imagined it was in. Huge golden gates are what they imagined and they were open. There was an edge at the entrance that looked like a bottomless pit. God still had not taken notice while we were moving toward the edge.

They put me down gently and I could feel the bones in my body shift with every movement. We knew we needed to sin in order to leave this horrible place and spend a lifetime with each other. A small lie should do it. Raziel looked at me and said. "I hate your marking."

My jaw shifted as the words I said slowly came out. "I hate your hair." Raziel put their hands on my waist and tried to slowly move us off the edge, but it was like a force was keeping us trapped in heaven. *Why will it not let us go through? Is it closed?*

Raziel shook their head. "Maybe it was not a big enough lie? Small lies could be okay in heaven. What can I say that is big enough?"

I looked directly into their eyes and I could tell they were panicking. *Calm my love calm. You can do this.* "Love." Tears were starting to form in their eyes and I knew they did not want to say it but would. Both of us would have to. *I just need to tell them I love them first.* Just as they were about to say it God turned to look at us. Jophiel's wings were a bit broken with a scar on their neck and their sword was out of their hands.

Time slowed at this moment as Raziel rushed to say it. "I do not love you." Slowly I tried to open my mouth, but my jaw clenched and I could not get any words out. *I need to tell them.* God raised their hand and the sword that Jophiel had was lifted into the air and thrown at me specifically. In that moment I studied the sword and the expressions of both God and Raziel. The sword that emitted that yellow color also had a bit of orange to show more determination. It was mixed in so light. Carvings were on the metal part of the sword yet I still did not know what they meant. God had a cold look. Their eyes were grey like ours but their eyebrows were furrowed. *How mad they must be.* I looked over finally toward Raziel. They were scared yet still had passion in their eyes. *I will remember your grey eyes that showed fire in them. I will remember that smile and your laugh. I will remember that marking we shared and the pain God put you through. Most importantly I will remember the love I share for you.* I closed my eyes ready for the pain until a thought was projected into my mind, "I will always love you."

I opened my eyes and time moved faster again. Everything happened so quickly. One moment I was closing my eyes and the next I was being shoved out of the way and Raziel's body was struck by the sword. It had struck their gut within a matter of moments. Our eyes locked, but soon they faded away into the bottomless pit since the force of the sword pushed them over the edge. "Save me please." Tears streamed from their eyes as they fell into the entrance. After the thought, I heard their scream. "MALACH!" *Now I understand why I heard you.* My heart shattered into a million different pieces. They were gone right in front of my eyes. They fell but were they alive? *How? How did this end so badly?* I looked over at God and saw them smiling while Jophiel was in shock.

An emotion started to rise in me and a power that I had not felt before was consuming me. Suddenly my body did not hurt anymore. It seemed as if the bones in my body had repaired themselves. I floated higher and higher. God motioned with their hand to pull me down, but it was no use. I was overpowering them. The loss of Raziel started to consume me. *I failed them. I lost them. I did not even say I love you.* God's grey interlocked with mine. *They did this. God did this. They shall die.* Somehow, I knew what to do. I opened my arms as if I almost embodied Jesus on the cross. Colors started to emit from my skin. It shined brightly around me, and the colors were so beautiful. They were like the colors in God's wings. "You killed the love of my life! Everyone shall remember the horror you put them through. You will die!" God may have been too stunned to speak, but they held a cold look with a smile on their face. *Their joy comes from the pain of others.* Jophiel's eyes were large, and they could not believe what was happening. *I am the prophet of heaven. I shall not fail my destiny.*

Before I could finally fulfill my destiny God flicked their hand. I had no idea what was coming at me until it hit me. I looked down and saw that Gabriel's sword had flown straight into my gut. *Just like Raziel.* Slowly I fell back to the ground. I looked up and saw God cock their head to the side. "Thought you could destroy me hm?" Behind them, Jophiel grabbed a little talisman they had hidden in their pocket and cupped their hands. The talisman was on a necklace and the pendant was a very small little circular shape. I could not see much of it but I could see a glimpse of a star and a jewel in the middle. It was yellow which signified that it did forever belong to Jophiel. Only they could use it. God made a cross-movement with their hand and slowly my eyes faded to black.

When I awoke, I was in God's home in the abyss where Cain transformed into Raziel. I tried to move my arm, but it was stuck to my side as if it was fused into my body. The only part of my body I could move was my eyes. To the left of me was a purple chair and an orange one while on the right was a red and green one. *The assigned seats of Archangels and Princes. The inner circle of God.* I knew I was in the center because in the center of my vision was the entrance. It was a huge round door that was hidden within the light. When it opened the light seemed to bend to show that it was a hidden entrance as if only the elite angels got to see the inside. No door handle was needed as it opened by the sound of a voice. A voice spoke from behind me. "You tried so hard." I could not see anything other than the shadow of the beautiful flow of colors. *God.* "You cannot speak and are completely weakened. How I love to see you in this state." The shadow started to get closer as God moved around the circle to face me straight on.

They were smiling, but I noticed that something was different on their face. A scar was across their cheek at this moment. It was not like the marking we shared, but as if something had happened. They noticed me staring at it. "Like it? Your friend Jophiel gave it to me. They tried too hard to save you after you blacked out, but unfortunately, they did not succeed. Their punishment shall come later. You are first. I cannot harm you, but I can take away what is most precious to you at this moment." My eyes widened at this. *They already took the love of my life away. I am already broken. Do your worst.* A small laugh escaped their mouth. "You are telling me to do my worst." *They can read my mind?* "Yes, I can. I always have been. All this time you told yourself how much you loved Raziel and that you wanted to fall together. I knew and so did Gabriel. You thought this was all a secret." *How did they find out?* "Jophiel. They planted hints to make sure you chose them. Gabriel was there at the bible reading area when you realized your feelings for Raziel." *The figure that floated away in the distance was Gabriel.* "They saw Jophiel with you two telling you how to fall. They saw everything because Jophiel told them. One small little plan to try to make you choose them." *How could they? Why would they tell Gabriel yet still try to save me?* "Because they need you to kill me." In a mocking voice, they said. "Bring freedom and joy to heaven!"

I could not believe everything I was hearing. *After all this time. I trusted them yet they betrayed me. They helped kill my love. I am truly troubled.* "Yes, Malach you are truly troubled You believe this because inside you know your destiny is not fulfilled. Soon you will be as pure as everyone else. The destiny will be but a rumor." Their smile grew bigger. *Ah, yes. This great thing you can take from me. I have failed at everything. What more can you do?* "Everything you learned can be gone in a second. The love you shared with Raziel can be gone. All I have to do is snap my fingers." *My memories. Recycle me all over again. Do it, I dare you.* They expected this from me. "I knew you would think that. I plan to, but this time Raziel will not be here to teach you. No one will. Jophiel cannot after I am done with them." *I will remember everything. My destiny and love are too strong.* They raised their right hand. "Goodbye Malach." All I saw was the snap of their fingers and the memory faded.

I was left in the black void and I was too stunned to speak about this. *I am somehow still alive for the purpose of God. I failed, yet where did Raziel go?* "Where did you go?" There was silence in the void. "Did you make it to Earth?" Still, there was no sound. Everything was so quiet. "Raziel?" My voice seemed to echo in the dark. Once my voice stopped everything was still. Suddenly a light shined in the distance of the void. I floated very quickly toward it. I was at its edge as it looked as if a hole was carved into the blackness. *Is this it?* I took one step closer and fell into the hole. *Please be my answer.*

Chapter Ten

As I entered the hole all I could think about was getting my answers. *I need to know if you are alive.* The light from the hole faded and I opened my eyes to see a blurry image of Sariel directly in my face. Everything was silent in my ears even though this dream state was different than the previous ones. While my vision started to go into focus, I was trying to process everything I had learned. *Raziel is possibly dead all because of God. However, Jophiel is also partly responsible. I need to know why the hell they betrayed me.* All my worries were about Raziel, but I did not let that consume me because of the hatred I felt for God. *I know what I need to do. My power was unlocked by the loss of Raziel. I wonder if I can channel that feeling and do it again, but more powerful this time and aware of my surroundings.* Sariel's voice interrupted my thoughts. "Malach wake up." They were being more like a mother towards me and the image of them finally focused. I smiled a bit at them until my eyes drifted toward a smiling Jophiel.

"Glad to see you awake. Did you finish the story?" The smile vanished from my face and all I could do was stare into their eyes. Slowly their smile faded. "You remembered. I can tell by your look. Let me explain." Emotions started to run throughout my body and I quickly got up letting my rage consume me while I grabbed the collar of Jophiel's clothing. Small light was emitting from my skin like it did before. They tensed up at seeing my power emerge and their eyes shifted between the light and my eyes. *How could you be a part of having killed my love?* Sariel was a little bit away from us but they were studying my skin. *They have no part in this.* Jophiel spoke. "Malach please let me explain. It is not like what you think."

My hands clenched harder on their collar. "How is it not? I remember every moment of their death. Then I remember God telling me that you planted hints for Gabriel and essentially told them about my love." Still, my eyes stayed interlocked with theirs. Sariel floated closer toward us and laid their hand on my arm. I looked into their eyes and it was calming to me.

"Stand down Malach. Let Jophiel explain. I am sure they have a reason or else they would not have saved your memories." Slowly I let go of Jophiel's collar and took Sariel's hands. Once I was calm I looked back at Jophiel.

"Explain please."

They nodded and started to tell their side. "Yes, I did plant hints to Gabriel. They started to find out at the beginning, but once Raziel admitted everything to you I realized what I did was wrong. I thought that by letting Gabriel know they would take Raziel away early on so that I could convince you to save heaven, but once you fell in love with each other I knew it was too late. The only thing I could do was not tell you how to fall. It was the last thing I had or the last thing heaven had to keep you here. I regret every moment of having helped in the loss of Raziel. Keeping your memories alive was the best thing I could do to hopefully redeem myself. The talisman protected them." Jophiel pulled out the necklace, I had seen in previous visions, from their pocket. It was a circular shape with the star of David on it with a yellow jewel in the middle. Such a small object could hold so much power. I nodded at them.

"I understand, but do not forgive you fully. Do you know what happened to Raziel after they fell?"

Jophiel shook their head. "After they fell I am not sure if they are alive or dead. Only God knows."

"I understand. We need to stop God now." I started to float away from them but Jophiel stopped me.

"You just remembered how to use your power. Maybe you should learn how to control it first?"

"I have waited too long. Who knows what happened to Raziel! They could be dead for all I know. I am determined to confront God and find out the answers." I kept trying to float away but with every inch I was trying to move Jophiel was blocking my way.

"Think about this first. If you are not prepared this time then God could erase your memories again. I am not sure if I could save them again."

"That does not matter. Finding out what happened to them is the only important thing now." I pushed Jophiel to the side, but they got in front of me again. Sariel was behind us following us. "Would you get out of my way?"

"Not until you stop and think about this."

I scoffed. "Like you thought about anything other than heaven when you told Gabriel?"

"I understand you are mad. Sorry is not something that can fix what happened."

"You are right. Sorry can not fix this. I can only get my answers now. God is the only one who can give them to me." Jophiel did not try to stop me this time, but Sariel did. Somehow while I was talking to Jophiel they got in front of us.

"Malach I think you should listen to Jophiel." I cared for Sariel, but I would not let them stand in my way. While I was trying to get around them they somehow knew my every move.

"Sariel please get out of my way. I need to know."

"Not until you think about this first."

"What is there to think about? Answers are the only thing I need now!" Even after I told them the truth they still got in my way. I was starting to get frustrated. "Sariel move!"

"No! What if you lose your memories again? Or die? How could heaven be saved without you? More importantly, how could you save Raziel if you are dead?"

My face softened at the idea of not being able to save Raziel. *Maybe they are right. I need to think about this. I am so determined to find my answers, but I could lose these memories again and Raziel may never be saved.* I let out a sigh and realized that they were right. Turning toward Jophiel I said, "What is our plan then?"

We all gathered together and moved away from the above just in case if Gabriel came down from the abyss. The best place for us to go was Raziel's and my spot. Since it was the farthest spot from prying eyes. We spent many moments there which gave me time to practice my powers. Somehow Jophiel had acquired their sword from the previous battle. *How did they get it back?* I learned from Jophiel that God could only move objects with their hands. So instead I learned how to move them with my mind. The hardest thing to learn was how to suppress God from reading my mind. This was one ability that God possessed that I did not have.

Jophiel was trying desperately to teach me. "You need to close off your mind. Imagine a wall blocking God's power."

I scoffed. "How is this going to work if I cannot practice it? No one here can read minds. I will not know if it worked till I am facing God themselves."

"We may not be able to practice it, but you will learn how to do it. You will know when the right moment is."

"How will I know when the right moment is?"

"You will just know. Now let's start again." I closed my eyes to begin. "Imagine that wall coming up to block God's power. Remember, in this moment you are no longer vulnerable. You have the strength to overcome God and defeat them once and for all. Nothing can penetrate that wall."

We kept practicing it over and over until I finally felt confident that I could stop them. During this time Sariel had come up with a plan for me to confront God. They said, "Now this could either end with us winning or us finding out that you are potentially dead." I nodded as I understood the risk I was taking. *I will try to save heaven, but my top priority is finding out what happened to Raziel. I need to know if I can save them.* Sariel continued telling us the plan in full. Before I left Jophiel had told me that God gave them their sword back as their payment for keeping quiet about what happened so then there was still order in heaven.

The moment had finally come for me to overtake God. Jophiel had given me their talisman in hopes that I could use some of its power to destroy God. I also had their sword by my side since Jophiel felt that the pair might help with my fight. *I feel like an Archangel in this moment.* Jophiel had told me where the entrance was to the abyss. In the above, it was hidden in the far depths and as I remembered from my vision there was a secret hidden door. It was in the blinding light above me. If you looked just right you could see the outline of it. Everything was white like the rest of heaven, but the door had a little outline that could only be seen when the little blue particles went over it. *I will get my answers and find you Raziel.* Sariel had mentioned that I needed to say a specific word for it to open. "Yahweh." *Most high.* Slowly the door started to creak open and the light seemed to bend. I floated up through the door into the abyss. When I entered I saw the door close and instead of being on the floor, it was behind me. *Strange.* In front of me was God's throne with the colored chairs around it but there was no God.

The closer I floated toward the throne the more nervous I got. My shoulders were tight and my breath was shallow and small. *Here is where everything happens. I will find out what happened.* I got close enough to actually touch the throne. My left hand moved to touch the gold that outlined the throne. *Power.* "Nice is it not?" I was startled by the voice and my left hand moved back to my side while my right gripped the holster that held Jophiel's sword. Slowly I turned my body to see God floating by the entrance. They had that same cocky smile I saw them with before. The scar was still on their cheek from the previous battle. "Too bad I could not get rid of it as it takes away from my pure form. That sword did that you know." I gripped the handle even harder. "When it pierces an angelic creature it becomes a scar immediately after. We can choose to get rid of it or keep it. For me, I wanted to remember how close you came last time, but then I want you to see it every time you lose. No matter how hard you try you will never beat me." *I will win and get my answers.* "You want the answer? Raziel is dead." *No.* They laughed as they could read my mind. I knew my every thought was being heard so I dared not tell them I could suppress them. I dared not try it yet as it was not the moment.

They floated closer toward me, but I drew Jophiel's sword. "That is far enough." I could feel my shoulders tense even more. I was ready to do this if needed.

They cocked their head to the side. That smile never left their face. "Such a strong front you are with that sword." With one hand they moved to throw it from my hand, but I kept that tight grip. My skin was starting to glow with a rainbow of colors. "Oh! Someone has learned." I was focused on their every move. I kept trying to make sure I would not think of my next move for fear of God knowing. "Why so quiet now?" They moved closer and I held my position. I could feel sweat starting to run down my forehead.

They took their left hand and made a fist. Suddenly my airway started to close from my throat. With their right hand, they lifted me up, but I still held on desperately to the sword. "You only learned one pathetic little trick. I have had many cycles to learn all of my tricks. You still have much to learn." I could feel my airway getting smaller and smaller. Imagining that wall I thought to myself. *Do something. Remember.* My breath started to get smaller and smaller till I could no longer breathe. "What a poor thing. You barely put up a fight.

My son, Lucifer put up a bigger fight than you." *Throw something!* I looked around and remembered all of the chairs around God's throne. While still trying to imagine that wall I picked up a chair behind God and threw it at them. They did not see it coming. *Do not think.* God stumbled and both their arms went down to their side. I fell onto the floor.

Gasping for breath I still somehow managed to hold onto the sword. God quickly regained their posture and stood up. I remembered I had the talisman in my pocket for extra power which I needed at this moment. Something new came out of God's hand. It looked like a bolt of light being shot directly at me. I managed to quickly grab the talisman from my pocket and shield myself with both items. The sword's blade had touched the talisman and created a sort of bubble of light around me that protected me. I was surprised at this. God was shocked by this, but it did not matter. In a swinging motion, both of their hands kept throwing bolts of light in my direction. I kept holding the talisman and sword together, but the bubble around me was losing strength quickly. Having imagined that wall I thought I could think freely. *The talisman and sword can only generate so much power. I need to channel my own to overpower them.* I took a deep breath and tried to channel my power into those two items, but it was not enough. Those balls of light kept hitting and hitting the bubble. *How?* Suddenly the bubble popped and I was left vulnerable. Both my body and mind were left for God to take.

God seemed to have gotten tired after that, but still kept that smile on their face. "Enough with these tricks Malach. You can only do so much." Thinking that my mind was free I started to think. *What can I do? Maybe throw chairs? Someone help, please.* Their laughter broke my thoughts. "There is nothing you can do and no one is here to help you. You could only suppress my ability for so long." They got closer and closer to me.

I decided that the only choice I had was to try to strike them. Slowly I got up and held the talisman by the handle of the sword to try to generate as much power as possible. I ran and tried to swing at God. I was aiming for their right hand. With their left, they tried to freeze me in place, but I was able to overpower them at that moment. I swung but they dodged out of the way in time. A bolt of light came at me from behind, but I quickly turned to shield that. God's back was now to their throne. With my mind, I took one of the chairs from behind them and threw it at them. They blasted that one away, but they could only do that so much. With my mind, I threw multiple chairs as they came flying at them until they finally knelt down which gave me enough time to run at them again, and with one swoop I chopped off their left hand. "AH! My HAND!" They could not decide to keep the scar or not as the power of the talisman and sword combined with my power was enough to overcome that choice.

I turned back quickly toward them with the two items gripped tightly in my hands. The light emitting from my skin was glowing brighter and brighter. Blood was dripping from God's left hand. The chopped hand had been tossed to the left side of God's throne. They turned slowly toward me and the smile had disappeared from their face. "You little demon. GABRIEL!" Their voice echoed throughout the room. "GABRIEL!" Everything was silent. They groaned in pain, but interlocked their eyes with mine. "Where are they?"

I smiled knowing that they were preoccupied. Sariel had mentioned in our plan that Gabriel needed to be dealt with so they decided to take the role. "Gabriel is with Sariel looking at 'pure' texts at this moment. They cannot answer your call."

God groaned even more. "You little bitch. No one can stop me! NO ONE!" Suddenly God started to emit with power of their own. Instead of a rainbow of colors, it was just one sold color. Gold. Their eyes changed from grey to gold as the power was starting to consume them. "You cannot beat the likes of me! You shall die like your lover."

They are not dead. "Yes, they are. They chose to die in that pit with the sword in their gut." *No.* "Yes Malach. They knew that no matter what they would still die. They never loved you." *You're wrong!* As God was rising so were the rest of the chairs in the abyss except for God's throne. Their right hand was lifting them up. "I am never wrong! My name is Yahweh and I am God. Creator of Earth and everyone. I will have ORDER!" As they said this all of the chairs flew toward me.

Time slowed at this moment. *God is wrong. They are not dead. They chose to survive. I will not obey their order. Everyone will remember what Yahweh did to them.* As the chairs got closer and closer the light from my skin got brighter and brighter. I let go of the sword and talisman in my right hand. I started to embody Jesus on the cross like I did before. *I will kill you.* My power started to shine throughout the abyss. The chairs that were inches away were destroyed and my eyes had changed to a rainbow of colors. *Raziel is alive and well on Earth. They still love me. I can feel them.* I was letting my thoughts run free at this moment. God needed to remember this moment. My power reached theirs and the golden light they emitted started to crack and crumble apart. "NO!" God screamed. Each crack got closer and closer to God's skin. "Malach stop. I will change the order, please! Do not kill me!"

I kept pressing closer and closer. "Tell me what I want to know then!"

The cracks started to run up to God's neck. "Stop please!"

I pressed my power harder and harder as I was channeling Raziel's love and loss all at the same time. "Tell me!"

The cracks were now around their mouth. "They are alive." My shoulders relaxed at finally knowing my answer, but I knew God could not live. I continued to let my power consume them. "No! Stop!" Those cracks shattered into a million particles. Rainbow colors were shining in those little particles. All the colors seemed to fall onto the golden star of David like snowflakes. *True beauty.*

Slowly I lowered myself onto the floor. God's throne was the only thing left in the abyss. Everything else was destroyed. Something was different though. I looked down at my arms and saw veins of color on my skin. *I consumed my power so much that it is a part of me now. I was never an Archangel. I was a Prince.* No one had ever seen the true power of a Prince. When a Prince used their power a flow of colors shined throughout their body. Since God was dead, I knew everything about heaven now. *God's power is mine now.* I knew what happened to Raziel and what was going to happen. *Before I can join them, I need to fix heaven.* I lifted my right hand and with a snap of my fingers, I was able to release all the memories that God erased back into the minds of all angels. Everything would be restored in heaven, but free will shall never be forgotten again.

I opened the door to the abyss with my mind and floated back into the above. Jophiel and Sariel were waiting for me. In the distance, Gabriel was floating. I smiled at both of them. Sariel floated quickly toward me and engulfed me in a big hug. Tears were streaming down their face, but they were happy ones. Slowly I moved back from our hug and took my right hand to cup their face. "Thank you for everything." Their smile was bigger than ever. "You can choose to stay or leave. No one will stop you now."

They nodded. "I want to go. I want to meet my human and tell them that everything will be okay." I smiled softly at them.

Sariel let go of me to let me see Jophiel. I put a hand on their shoulder. "I will forgive you if you do one thing."

They nodded. "Anything Malach."

"Lead heaven through this tough time. Chaos will ensue, but you know how things need to be. Make sure all angels know they have a choice. Falling does not require a lie anymore. They can choose to leave and come back whenever they please."

A tear started to trickle down their cheek. "I will. Freedom will forever be known in heaven." I nodded and slowly made my way toward Gabriel.

They did not look happy or sad at this moment. "Gabriel."

"What do you want now? You got what you wanted. Chaos in heaven."

I shook my head. "Not chaos, but freedom. Learn how to be human. It is the only way now."

They scoffed and I left them to their thoughts. *I can only do so much.* Colors were shining everywhere in heaven. Everything that was once known previously was now in the present. I flew down from the above over toward the entrance of heaven. Souls that were entering were in amazement at how beautiful everything was. They could now join their loved ones in heaven or have a chance to become an angel. I made sure everyone had a choice. By the entrance, I looked down into the pit. For the first time, I had a choice of staying or leaving. I looked around at everything I had changed. *Everything is so beautiful now. I can finally choose to stay or leave. It is my choice. Leave or stay? My lover is waiting for me down on Earth. I know heaven will always be waiting for me to return.* I was glad to have a choice. Since I retained some of God's ability I knew where Raziel was and who they were on Earth. *They have such a beautiful name. I cannot wait to see them and say their name. The sweet and charming name. The one that makes me full of joy. Rory, I shall see you soon.* After taking in the changed world around I finally made my choice. "I choose to go to my love. I will always remember what happened here. Do not miss me too much."

Looking back down into the pit I took one step and fell in. The blackness surrounded me until I saw a blinding light like the dream state, but this time was different. When I opened my eyes, I saw a woman in front of me smiling. She had long brown hair with a hint of red in it that was messy at this particular moment. Looking around I noticed the ceiling was white, but the walls were a mixture of pink and blue. I looked back at the woman and saw small drops of sweat dripping from her forehead which had some wrinkles that were just starting to show, but then my eyes drifted toward hers. They were a darker green on the outer but got brighter the closer the color got to the pupil. A dimple was on her cheek as she smiled. Her lips were full, but her teeth were not pure white. Small bits of yellow stained her teeth. Moving my eyes from her face I noticed she was sitting in some sort of bed that was covered with a bleached white sheet. Wrinkles were on the sheet as if she struggled for some reason on it. A blue blanket is what I was wrapped in. Everything on my skin was very soft and warm. This made me realize that her hand was rubbing my forehead down to my cheek which was calming. Her hand was soft against my skin. My eyes shifted to look at the hand as it seemed to be as big as my entire head. Small tears were running down her cheeks as I looked into her eyes. When she spoke, she had a honeyed tone of voice. "Welcome to the world Malachai."

Don't miss out!

Visit the website below and you can sign up to receive emails whenever Maximilienne Montana publishes a new book. There's no charge and no obligation.

https://books2read.com/r/B-A-MLRIC-ZDMWE

BOOKS 2 READ

Connecting independent readers to independent writers.

www.ingramcontent.com/pod-product-compliance
Lightning Source LLC
Chambersburg PA
CBHW031755150726
47989CB00006B/2731